All Must Die

I.J. Parnham

A Black Horse Western

ROBERT HALE · LONDON

© I.J. Parnham 2015
First published in Great Britain 2015

ISBN 978-0-7198-1541-6

Robert Hale Limited
Clerkenwell House
Clerkenwell Green
London EC1R 0HT

www.halebooks.com

The right of I.J. Parnham to be identified as
author of this work has been asserted by him
in accordance with the Copyright, Designs and
Patents Act 1988

Typeset by
Derek Doyle & Associates, Shaw Heath
Printed and bound in Great Britain by
CPI Antony Rowe, Chippenham and Eastbourne

CHAPTER 1

The first two gunshots were wild, but the third shot sliced into the top of the boulder.

Sheriff Cassidy Yates ducked down, fast-crawled along the ground, and then got up on his haunches ten feet away. Three rapid gunshots tore out, but thankfully they were all aimed at his former position giving him enough time to understand the situation.

He dropped back down and beckoned Deputy Hearst to join him.

'Our quarry has gone to ground between two boulders thirty feet away,' Cassidy said, while pointing. 'The shooters who ambushed us are up on the ridge and they have a clear view of the area.'

'Which just leaves the question of who these gunmen are. Klaude never gave the impression he had any friends in Monotony.'

Cassidy nodded. Then, testing a theory, he rose up.

Klaude Stern was peering up the ridge towards the shooters' position, and this time the gunfire that had made the two lawmen scurry into hiding didn't erupt.

'Perhaps we got it wrong,' Cassidy said, ducking down. 'The shooters might not be friends of his.'

'But they could be friends of Hamilton Davenport,' Hearst said, completing the thought.

Last month, Hamilton had ridden into town looking for work. He'd been rough-clad and surly, so he'd had no success. While drowning his sorrows in the Two Bit saloon, he'd taken exception to a man who was celebrating finding work.

With no provocation Hamilton had shot him, so the case against Hamilton had been clear cut. He'd received a life term.

He had been thrown in the jailhouse where he had waited to be taken to Beaver Ridge jail, but a week ago he had been found lying dead beside his cot. The other two prisoners in his cell backed up each other's story that Hamilton had tripped up and banged his head on the bars.

They'd kept to that story and the facts appeared to support them. There were no marks on Hamilton's body other than a livid bruise on the side of his head.

The two prisoners had only been locked up for a drunken fight and so they had been released with a warning not to leave town until Cassidy had completed the investigation into Hamilton's demise.

One man, Laidley Rose, was a citizen of Monotony and he'd complied, but Klaude Stern was an itinerant worker and he'd taken the first chance to flee.

Klaude had reached Spinner's Gulch before the lawmen caught up with him, but they'd all ridden into an ambush.

'You men up on the ridge,' Cassidy shouted. 'You're not handing out justice to this man today. Leave now and let the law decide if he's committed a crime.'

Any hope that the shooters would listen to sense fled when a volley of gunshots tore out. The shots, their ricochets and the echoes created a continuous burst of noise, making it sound as if an army had ambushed them.

When Cassidy noted that none of the gunfire was being directed at them, he moved on behind the line of covering boulders. At the endmost boulder, he glanced around the side and found that Klaude had tried to flee, but he hadn't got far.

He was lying on his chest with a blooded lower back and a bleeding right leg. He was struggling to drag himself forward and his weak movements suggested he wouldn't survive.

Cassidy grunted in irritation. Then, with Hearst at his side, he edged out into clear space.

With their target breathing his last, he expected the shooters would now make good their escape, and accordingly he halved the distance to the shot man without reprisals. Then a gunshot tore out, picking out Klaude's back and making him arch his body before he slammed down on the ground.

With Klaude now lying still, Cassidy hunkered down, but he couldn't see where the shooter had fired from. When a minute passed without further gunfire, he moved on to the body.

He turned Klaude over and the man flopped over, his eyes blank. Hearst stood with his gun trained on the ridge and so Cassidy turned away, but then a wheezing murmur emerged from Klaude's lips.

'A piece of work,' he breathed.

With one eye on the ridge, Cassidy dropped to his knees beside him.

'What are you trying to say?' he asked, as Klaude continued to mumble.

'In action. . . .' Klaude trailed off. Then his head lolled to the side.

A long expulsion of air blew dust across the ground followed by silence. Even when Cassidy shook his shoulder, Klaude didn't breathe again.

'I didn't hear that,' Hearst said, edging towards him.

'He was babbling. I don't reckon—'

A ferocious volley of gunshots cut off Cassidy's comment and in self-preservation both men hurried towards the boulders where Klaude had holed up earlier. Another burst of gunfire sped them on their way and, unlike before, the shots sounded as if they were coming from several directions, and the shooters were closer.

'Those gunmen sure don't want anyone to walk away from this,' Hearst said.

'Then that's their mistake,' Cassidy said.

Hearst grunted that he agreed and then he moved to stand at the side of the entrance into the gap while Cassidy stood on the other. With their mission having failed and with them facing an unknown number of gunmen, they waited for their adversaries to make the first move.

Ten minutes passed in silence and Cassidy was starting to think that the shooters had left when someone shouted a warning over to his left. Then gunfire ripped out, coming from behind them as well as from both sides.

'Surrounded,' Hearst muttered unhappily.

'We sure are,' Cassidy said, 'but stay put and let the gunmen come to us.'

Cassidy steadied his arm against the side of the boulder as he prepared to take the first man to come into sight, but sporadic gunfire continued to rattle away without anyone becoming visible. Neither did he see where the bullets landed.

With each new volley the thought grew that, like before, they weren't the principal targets. So he wasn't surprised when, after a lull in the firing, someone called to them close to the position where they'd first gone to ground.

'Hey, you two over by the rocks,' the man shouted. 'I reckon you can come out now. It looks as if we've seen them off.'

Hearst glanced at Cassidy, his raised eyebrows questioning if he thought this was a trick. Cassidy shrugged, but with only one way to find out, he edged into the open to find that a man was standing in clear view on the other side of Klaude's body.

He was tall with an easy smile and with his gun held low, although the smile died when he moved closer to the fallen man.

'I don't reckon we had much to do with getting rid of them,' Cassidy called. 'You were doing all the shooting.'

'I just finished what you started.' The man pointed up the ridge. 'I saw three men hightail it away towards Monotony.'

'You see enough to recognize them if you saw them again?'

The man started to shake his head, but when Hearst came out to join him, he flinched and then tipped back his hat.

'You're both lawmen.'

'Sure. And you?'

'The name's Marcel Cartwright. I was heading to Monotony to look for work when I heard a whole mess of shooting going on.'

'And you decided to defend the people being shot at.'

Marcel laughed and moved on to join them.

'In my experience, those are the people to side with.'

Cassidy glanced at Hearst, who provided an encouraging nod.

'So you've had some experience of defending people in trouble, have you?'

'Some.'

Cassidy appraised the man, who smiled as he clearly picked up on the likely direction of this conversation.

'You ever thought about being a deputy lawman?'

'I was once deputized, for a short time. Are you offering something more permanent?'

'Hearst and me have provided enough law for the townsfolk of Monotony, but the town's growing and that means we're getting more trouble. We've even got a new jailhouse now.'

Cassidy held out his hand and Marcel moved forward to take it.

'In that case,' he said, 'you'll need another lawman to help you fill it.'

CHAPTER 2

'I've found no sign of Laidley Rose,' Hearst said when he met up with Cassidy in the law office in the early evening. 'And nobody knows where he's gone.'

Laidley was the other man who had been in Hamilton Davenport's cell when he'd died. Cassidy's first priority when they'd returned to town had been to find him and see if Klaude's demise might shake more information out of him.

As Hearst knew the town, Cassidy had given his new deputy the task of following the gunmen's trail, a task he'd accepted with relish.

'It's too early to get concerned yet,' Cassidy said, sitting back in his chair. 'But after what happened to Klaude, what do you think happened to Hamilton?'

Hearst shrugged. 'I saw nothing to suggest it wasn't an accident.'

'Agreed, but even though Klaude knew that was the way we were thinking, he hightailed it out of here, and he must have had good reason because he got shot up.'

'Either way, they were the only witnesses and so if we can't find Laidley, the truth will probably never emerge.'

Cassidy nodded. Then the two men sat in pensive silence until the new deputy returned.

'I picked up the gunmen's trail and followed them towards town,' Marcel reported. 'They looked as if they were hell-bent on causing more trouble. With it getting dark I came back to get help.'

Cassidy smiled. 'That sounds like a mighty successful first day as a lawman. Where did you last see them?'

'They were near this large house a mile out of town.'

Marcel pointed to the east, making Cassidy and Hearst nod.

'That's Horace Franklyn's spread,' Hearst said. 'And he's one of the wealthiest men in town.'

'Then that probably explains what they were doing,' Marcel said. 'It looked as if they were watching the place and planning to break in.'

Without further discussion the three men headed outside and mounted up. As they rode out of town, Marcel explained that he'd seen the gunmen on a rise that looked down on the house, although when they approached the rise, the men were no longer there.

With Horace's safety paramount, they rode

13

directly to the house. Hearst was riding up front and when the house came into view, he turned in the saddle.

'I reckon the trouble's already started,' he said.

Cassidy hurried on to join Hearst and he had to agree. Horace was a private man who usually kept his own company in the evening, and yet lights were burning in all his rooms and the shadows of several people were moving quickly behind the shutters in the main room.

'Let's hope we're not too late,' Cassidy said.

The three men dismounted beside the barn. Cassidy ordered Marcel to stay outside and await developments while he beckoned Hearst to join him in hurrying on to the house.

The two lawmen stopped on either side of the door, where they listened. Subdued conversation was coming from the main room, but Cassidy couldn't make out what was being said.

He had been to Horace's house before, so he knew that a corridor ran the length of the house and that there were two entrances into the main room. He backhanded the front door open and when the corridor turned out to be unoccupied, he and Hearst slipped inside and took one door apiece.

Again they listened and again Cassidy couldn't make out what was being said, but the tones were animated and one of the voices was a woman's. Concerned now about the situation they would face, he caught Hearst's eye.

14

When Hearst nodded, he raised three fingers on his left hand while drawing his gun. He lowered his fingers in a rapid countdown.

Then in a co-ordinated move he and Hearst burst through. Cassidy hurried two steps to the side and, with his back to the wall, he faced the room.

'Everyone put their hands where I can. . . .' Cassidy trailed off when four sets of eyes jerked round to look at him. They were all shocked, and were all female.

The women were seated facing the front of the room where three screens had been placed so that they could see what was happening within the square area created by the screens. This area wasn't visible to Cassidy and so in bemusement he glanced at Hearst, who could see the whole room, although his raised eyebrows and furrowed brow didn't provide any answers.

Cassidy edged a pace closer revealing Horace standing over Josephine Updike, the wife of the owner of the Two Bit saloon. She was lying on her back on a low table and an open case was on a chair beside her. The case contained two cylindrical metal objects while Horace held two short wooden handles that were connected to the cylinders.

Cassidy couldn't work out what the metal or wooden objects were, but as Horace appeared to be aiming the handles at Josephine, he turned his gun on Horace, which made him bristle with indignation.

' "When sorrows come," ' Horace said, eyeing Cassidy and then Hearst, ' "they come not single spies but in battalions." '

Horace's obvious surprise and Josephine's wide-open eyes that appeared more concerned with Cassidy's arrival than with whatever Horace was doing to her made him lower his gun.

'Some men were acting suspiciously nearby,' Cassidy said. 'I thought they might have broken in.'

Horace spread his hands to hold the two handles wide apart.

'Can you see those men in here?'

'I can't.' Cassidy frowned and the thought came that if the men hadn't been planning a robbery, they might have had a different motive. 'Is Laidley Rose here?'

'I don't believe I've ever spoken to Laidley.'

Cassidy nodded. 'We'll check around outside – there's no need to be alarmed.'

'You're the only ones causing alarm.'

'I can see that.' Cassidy turned to the assembled women and tipped his hat, but that only made them glower and so he looked again at the case, but he couldn't work out what Horace was doing with it. 'I'll leave you to carry on doing . . . whatever it is you're doing.'

Cassidy waited, but when no explanation was forthcoming, he collected Hearst and they headed into the corridor. Once they were outside, Hearst considered him with a sly smile, but Cassidy didn't find the situation amusing enough to return it.

When they joined Marcel, he directed him to scout around the rise while he and Hearst checked out the immediate vicinity. They split up and took either side of the house, but when the three men met up fifteen minutes later, none of the lawmen had found any sign of anything untoward.

'I reckon the gunmen moved on,' Marcel said. 'In the dark, I doubt we'll be able to pick up their trail again.'

'I agree,' Cassidy said, peering into the darkness, 'but if they didn't show up here, it makes me wonder where they are now.'

'I've told you everything I know,' Barney Rose whined.

'Your everything isn't enough,' Renard Icke muttered. He leaned over the counter and grabbed Barney's collar. 'You know where your brother's gone to ground.'

Barney gulped as Renard drew him up close and he couldn't meet his eyes, making Renard snarl with irritation. Renard dragged him up on to the counter and then over it, making him thud to the floor on his back.

Renard waited until Barney moved to rise and then kicked out, his boot connecting squarely with Barney's chin, poleaxing him. He stalked around Barney's still form, waiting for him to gather the strength to get back up, while his two men continued their systematic ransacking of the trading post.

It was clear that Laidley wasn't hiding here. On the other hand, Volney Atwell had found a few dollars beneath the counter and Ossie Byers had found a wad of bills in Barney's storeroom.

Barney's lack of anguish after both discoveries convinced Renard that the well-being of his brother was more important to him than the loss of his money, and that suggested he was still holding out on him. So when Barney rolled on to his knees and then crawled towards the door, Renard slapped both hands on Barney's back.

He dragged him off the floor and threw him across the post. Barney wheeled into a pile of corn sacks, tipping them over.

When Barney came to rest, he was lying sprawled over two sacks. Renard stood over him with one foot raised, but Barney still mustered a defiant glare up at him.

'You can throw me around the post all evening,' Barney said, 'but I still won't have any idea where Laidley is.'

'Obliged for the offer,' Renard said with a smirk.

He reached down to grab Barney, but then his growing irritation with the situation got the better of him. Feeling tired with a process that had gone on for longer than he'd expected, he slapped the sole of his boot against Barney's hip and shoved him over.

Several poles were standing propped up in a pail.

He selected one and then clattered it down over Barney's back.

The pole made a satisfying whistling sound followed by a thud and so heartened he repeated the process, breaking the pole over Barney's shoulders. He grabbed a second, but that one broke on the first swipe, destroying his brief good mood.

He picked up the pail, hurled the remaining poles over his shoulder, and then hammered the pail down on the back of Barney's head. Without making a sound Barney slumped and with his anger assuaged, Renard fingered the dent in the pail before tossing it aside.

'We could tear this place apart,' Ossie said, breaking off from his rummaging, 'but unless Barney talks, we won't get any closer to Laidley.'

'From the look of the dent in that pail,' Volney said, 'he won't be talking much.' Both men looked at Renard for guidance.

Renard moved around the still trading-post owner. He didn't want to admit he might have gone too far, so he laughed.

'He's just resting,' he said. 'We need to motivate him more. So torch this place.'

His two men chortled at this plan and scurried off to do his bidding, but Barney didn't react. Renard slumped down on a corn sack beside him and waited for him to stir, giving him plenty of encouragement by shouting out unneeded orders to the other two men.

Barney didn't stir even when they poured liquor over a pile of cloth and got a roaring fire started. Within moments the fire spread to a pile of empty sacks and then beyond, making the two men dance back.

They shot worried glances at each other. Then Volney hurried to the door while Ossie came over to join Renard.

'If he's not worried by this fire, he's not feigning being out cold,' he said.

'I know.' Renard stood up and glanced around the post that was now bathed in harsh light. 'The worst thing about all this is, I don't reckon he was holding out on us after all.'

Renard waited until Ossie snorted a laugh and then followed Volney, aiming to leave the building before the flames spread too far.

'Aren't you taking him with us?' Ossie called after him. 'This place is going to burn down quickly.'

'You want to bring him, you're carrying him,' Renard said without turning.

Ossie muttered under his breath, but rustling sounded as he presumably took hold of Barney. Renard had reached the door when a crack sounded above his head.

He ducked and leapt into the doorway, but the cracking continued and a heavy thud sounded. Renard whirled round to see that the trading post was even more ramshackle than he'd thought; a supporting timber had fallen from the ceiling and it was now standing at an angle in the centre of the room.

Ossie was struggling to drag the comatose Barney past the end of the timber while the rush of air flared the flames. Renard reckoned that within moments the whole place would be ablaze and so he scrambled out through the door.

Outside, Volney had already mounted up and he was waiting with their horses as he prepared to leave quickly. He glanced at Renard before looking around, suggesting he thought the fire would soon attract interest from the nearby Monotony.

As another thud sounded in the post, Renard moved on to the horses.

'Ossie had better hurry up,' Volney called.

Renard was minded to teach Ossie a lesson by abandoning him, but the thought came that being moved might have livened up Barney and he'd be so grateful he'd talk about Laidley.

While he still had the chance to help, Renard hurried back to the door, but when he peered inside he saw that he was already too late to gain anything more out of this situation. Flames were licking at all four walls and, worse, the second thud had been caused by another timber dropping down and this one had trapped both Ossie and Barney beneath it.

Barney wasn't moving, but Ossie was sitting up and straining to shove the timber off his trapped legs. When he saw Renard, he gestured at him.

21

'Help me!' he shouted. 'I reckon I've broken my leg.'

Renard glanced around and confirmed that the route to the door would remain free for at least another minute and that no more heavy objects were likely to fall from the roof. He edged inside.

'Seems to me that you shouldn't have tried to help Barney,' he said.

'This isn't the time to gloat.'

Renard appraised the timber, noting that it wasn't moving because it was wedged against a box and Ossie only had to push the box aside to dislodge the timber.

Renard shrugged. 'I've got nothing to gloat about. I'm no closer to finding Laidley and I only got a hundred dollars out of this.'

'That's not enough to make it worth leaving me here. Help me.'

'You've been useful to me, so I guess I should help you.' Renard waited until Ossie sighed with relief, and then drew his gun. He sighted Ossie's head. 'I'll make this quick.'

'No!' Ossie shouted, cringing away.

'I assume that means you don't want my help, then.'

Renard waited until Ossie glared at him with an incredulous look and then tipped his hat. With an easy stroll, he headed to the door.

Behind him, Ossie started screaming and a few moments later, Barney screamed, too. So by the time Renard slipped outside he was smiling.

CHAPTER 3

'At least we know where those gunmen went last night,' Hearst said, pointing at the prints that showed three horses had passed this way.

'It looks as if they weren't interested in robbing Horace Franklyn, only in finding Laidley Rose,' Cassidy said, shaking his head sadly.

Late last night Horace had still been spooked and so he'd checked that nobody was lurking near his house. Nobody had been, but he'd spotted the fire.

By the time help arrived, the blaze was already out of control and it hadn't been possible to save the trading post or Barney, who was lying dead on the ground outside. He had been shot repeatedly in the chest.

At first light the lawmen had scouted around and they'd found a survivor of the blaze. He'd dragged himself away, but with a broken leg and several nasty burns he hadn't got far.

Marcel was helping Doc Taylor get the injured

man back to Monotony. The man's guarded answers and his failure to provide a name suggested that the fire had been deliberate and that he'd been involved.

Hearst moved away and then came to a sudden halt.

'What do you make of this?' he asked.

He pointed down. Cassidy joined him to find that someone had etched out a word on the ground, perhaps with the heel of their boot.

'How?' Cassidy said, reading the word. 'Which begs the question of why would someone write that?'

'The message could have been longer, but the rest got rubbed away.'

Cassidy shook his head. 'You're assuming that someone involved in the fire wrote this, but it could be anyone.'

Both men shrugged and then, with neither man offering any further suggestions, they headed back to Monotony. When they rode back into town, they called in on Doc Taylor, who had finished splinting the survivor's leg and dressing his burns.

Taylor drew Cassidy away from the infirmary door and reported that Marcel had left him on the edge of town so that he could search for the culprits' trail. Cassidy hadn't ordered Marcel to do this, but he was pleased that his new deputy was using his initiative.

'By the time we reached town the pain had loosened the injured man's tongue,' Taylor said. 'He's provided the name of Ossie Byers and, as you thought, the men who burned down the trading post were looking for Laidley. Ossie claimed Barney's death was an accident and he got him out, but he still died.'

'The name means nothing to me,' Cassidy said. 'But does that story sound plausible to you?'

'With all those bullets in Barney's chest, he stood no chance.'

Cassidy nodded and then moved on.

'I hear that you were brave last night,' he called out as he and Hearst entered the surgery.

Ossie was lying on a bed and he turned with a smile on his lips that died when he saw who had come in.

'I tried to save Barney,' he murmured while not looking at Cassidy. 'I got him out and he was alive when I left him, but he must have been injured worse than I thought.'

'He sure was. I counted at least six bullets in him.'

'I never saw him get shot up.'

'You expect me to believe that?' Cassidy waited for a response. When one wasn't forthcoming, he moved around the bed to stand in Ossie's eyeline. 'So who started the fire?'

'I don't know.'

'Three men ambushed us in Spinner's Gulch yesterday and they shot up Klaude Stern.'

'I've never been to Spinner's Gulch.'

'Those same three men were then followed to town where they were seen loitering around suspiciously in the dark.'

'I don't know nothing about that either.'

'Then three riders arrived at the trading—'

'I said that I don't know nothing about nothing that happened yesterday,' Ossie snapped, as Cassidy's questions finally irritated him.

'So what were you doing yesterday?'

'Trying to help a man escape from a burning building.'

'While the other two men left you to die, and they presumably killed Barney in the hope that you'd get the blame.' Cassidy smiled when Ossie's eyes flared, confirming he was getting close to the truth. 'Who were they?'

Ossie opened his mouth, but then made an obvious show of clamping it shut. Cassidy shook his head and then glanced at Hearst.

'Doc Taylor says he's fit to leave,' Hearst said.

'That's good,' Cassidy said, when Ossie sighed with relief. 'He can do his resting up in the jail-house. Make sure he gets the best possible care.'

'Hey,' Ossie grunted.

Cassidy turned away, leaving Hearst to deal with him, but he stopped at the door.

'I'll visit the prisoner again later, Deputy Hearst. Before I decide what charges he'll face, I'd welcome hearing two names.'

Cassidy waited and, as he'd hoped, with a resigned groan Ossie spoke up.

'Renard Icke left me to die in the trading post,'

he said. 'Volney Atwell didn't help me none, but he just does what Renard tells him to do.'

'Obliged,' Cassidy said, although the names weren't familiar to him. 'You continue being that co-operative when I return, you and I will get on just fine.'

With that, he moved on and tried to complete his understanding of last night's events. That required him to offer two apologies, and he sought out Josephine Updike in the Two Bit saloon.

As it turned out, he found he could provide both apologies at the same time, as Horace Franklyn was drinking coffee at the bar while Josephine was wiping down tables.

'You have nothing to apologize about,' Horace said, his tone low and gruff. 'You were just doing your duty.'

Cassidy nodded and turned to Josephine, but she muttered something to herself and then hurried behind the bar leaving half the tables untouched.

'And I'm sorry if I embarrassed you,' Cassidy called after her, but she didn't break her stride as she headed into a back room, forcing him to make his last words for Horace's ears only. 'Even if I have no idea what you were doing.'

The case Horace had set out last night was on the bar beside him, except this morning it was closed. Cassidy gave it a significant look.

' "The lady doth protest too much, methinks," ' Horace said. 'But she's clearly concerned, and I'd guess the rest of the ladies might be slow in coming to see me again, too.'

Horace opened up the case to let Cassidy see inside, even though that didn't help him.

'Some kind of telegraph machine?' Cassidy guessed.

'It sends messages, of a kind.'

Horace held out one of the wooden handles to Cassidy, who noted that a strip of metal was at the end. With a shrug he took hold of the handle.

Even though Horace's hand was still, when Cassidy touched the metal, it felt like it kicked against his fingers. The surprising effect jolted his hand and made him utter an involuntary oath that made Horace smile.

'What was that?' Cassidy said, drawing back his hand.

'The future.' Horace put the handle back in the case. 'That was electricity and one day soon it'll transform all our lives.'

'How will a metal strip that bites transform any-thing?' Cassidy said, wringing his hand.

'Because it made you perform an involuntary movement: you drew back your hand.'

Cassidy shrugged. 'I could stamp on your foot and that'd make you perform an involuntary move-ment, too.'

Horace closed the case with a firm click.

'You'll stop scoffing when I'm at the forefront of the revolution.'

Cassidy was minded to scoff some more as he was sure Horace was just quoting the words that had been uttered by whoever had sold him this contraption. But Horace had suffered enough over the last few years and he appeared enthused by his acquisition.

'What revolution?' he asked, reckoning he'd struggle to appear interested if he asked a longer question.

'This device makes the body react even when it doesn't want to, which means it can treat a variety of maladies that Doc Taylor could never cure.'

'Ah!' Cassidy murmured. 'In that case I could hazard a guess about what you were doing last night, and why my unexpected arrival angered Josephine and the other women.'

'Sure, although we'd all be grateful if you didn't guess.' Horace shuffled his stool closer. 'On the other hand, you could guess all day and you'd never mention everything this device could cure. It can resolve ailments not just of the body, but nervous complaints of the mind and, if the soul be full of discord and dismay, maybe that, too.'

'That sure is a lot of maladies.'

Cassidy backed away for a pace, now eager to move on and to avoid getting caught up in something that had captured Horace's imagination but which didn't interest him. Horace considered him and he was astute enough to pick up on his mood as his shoulders slumped.

'Please forgive my enthusiasm. I accept I'm exploring the possibilities only because it takes my mind off other matters.'

'It must be a year now since Gertie died.' Cassidy offered an encouraging smile. 'We all miss her.'

'It'll be a year next week, but that's not what's on my mind. Sykes Caine, the man who killed her, came out of jail last month. Earlier this week he was seen in Prudence.' Horace bunched a fist. 'It looked as if he was heading this way.'

'Tell me about Sykes Caine,' Cassidy said.

Tormond Quincy frowned and he took a short walk back and forth along his porch. When he stopped he faced the twilight redness on the horizon.

'I hoped I'd never have to hear that name again,' he said with a heavy tone.

'Horace Franklyn says Sykes might be coming here.'

'It wouldn't surprise me. That man never would listen to sense.'

Tormond embarked on another slow walk back and forth. Cassidy let him take his time in choosing the right words.

Tormond was a former sheriff of Monotony and in his early days of being a lawman Cassidy had often sought his aid. Those days were infrequent now, but despite the situation, Cassidy enjoyed having a reason to seek him out again.

'I've heard a few people mention him over the years, but all I know is he killed Horace's daughter Availia. Sadly, Horace also blames his wife's death on Sykes.'

'That's understandable. Gertie never was right again after Availia's death. It was a blessing when death released her from her suffering.'

Cassidy nodded, now seeing why Horace's electrical contraption might have interested him. He said it could cure nervous complaints, and that would describe the pains his wife had suffered. So perhaps he had bought it in the hope that he could stop others from suffering as she had.

'Then let's hope Horace doesn't have to suffer Sykes's presence again.'

Tormond nodded. 'Sykes was the worst case I ever had to deal with and I had many contenders. Three bodies were found in as many weeks. He was connected to all the dead people, but I never once thought him responsible.'

'He must have been devious to avoid your justice.'

'I'd like to think so, but in truth he was my one failure.' Tormond lowered his head with his eyes troubled as he clearly recalled the events. 'Each person had been shot repeatedly and dumped outside town. Beside their bodies were odd messages scrawled on the ground.'

Cassidy gulped. 'What kind of messages?'

Tormond shrugged. 'He wrote one word at the

scene of the first crime, and then added a second and a third word, but even then it still made no sense. I'd guess I stopped him before he completed whatever he wanted to say.'

'So what did the three words say?'

Tormond narrowed his eyes as he thought back.

'All that live.'

'Like you say, it don't make no sense.' Cassidy thought back to the one-word message at the trading post that he had dismissed as irrelevant along with Barney's bullet-ridden body. 'Yesterday a man called Renard Icke killed Klaude Stern. Then he burned down Barney Rose's trading post and shot up Barney while searching for his brother Laidley. Does that sound like something Sykes could be involved with?'

'Sykes worked alone.'

Cassidy nodded. 'Thankfully in the end you must have worked out what he was doing. Sykes has been in jail for the last ten years.'

'But not as punishment for the people he killed.' Tormond stopped his pacing to face Cassidy. 'He always had money on him and it turned out that he had a hidden stash, all stolen during a bank raid in Prudence. It was enough to get him ten years.'

'So why were you sure that Sykes was the killer, too?'

'Because the bodies stopped turning up.'

The two men considered each other.

'Now it's ten years later, Sykes is a free man again,

and he could be heading here.' Cassidy patted Tormond's shoulder. 'So keep a lookout for trouble.'

'I'm a former lawman: I always sleep with one eye open.' Tormond frowned. 'But if Sykes returns, a lot more people will be doing that.'

CHAPTER 4

'Search the records for anything you can find out about Sykes Caine,' Cassidy said when he arrived at the law office early that afternoon.

Cassidy had gone to the burnt-out trading post to search for Renard's trail, but overnight rain had flattened the ground as well as washing away the one-word message outside the post.

'You reckon he's involved in the recent trouble?' Deputy Hearst asked.

'Tormond Quincy doesn't think so, but he said that Sykes scrawled cryptic messages on the ground at the scenes of his crimes and he used to repeatedly shoot his victims. So I have a hunch that Renard Icke and Sykes Caine will link up somehow.'

Hearst nodded. 'While I do that, you need to check something out: Doc Taylor's just left the jailhouse and he says there was more trouble there last night.'

Cassidy nodded and moved to leave, but then

turned back.

'I could do that, but I keep forgetting I now have two deputies. I could get Marcel to check out the details.'

'You could, but only if you can find him. He left town to look for Renard earlier.'

Cassidy sighed. 'What do you make of your new colleague?'

'I haven't spent enough time with him to answer that, but I guess that means he's taking his duties seriously.'

Cassidy laughed at Hearst's guarded answer.

'There's a fine line between taking the initiative and being a loose cannon. He can't have spent more than five minutes on duty in Monotony since he arrived, and I'd prefer my new deputy to learn about the town.'

'He's taken a room in the Shaw Hotel.' Hearst frowned. 'If he doesn't check back with you today, I'll have a word with him.'

Cassidy nodded and then left the law office. When he arrived at the jailhouse, he found that Taylor hadn't exaggerated the situation: Ossie Byers was dead.

The outlaw was lying beside his cot. The jailer, Webster Todd, hadn't moved him since he'd found him, the only change being his shirt having been ripped open when Taylor had tried to help him.

'Taylor reckons Ossie must have been more injured than he thought,' Webster said, standing in the cell doorway.

Cassidy sat on the cot and considered the body. Livid burns covered Ossie's chest in addition to his bandaged arms and splinted leg, but he couldn't help but note the circumstance was similar to Hamilton Davenport's death.

'He sure looks in a bad way.' Cassidy looked up at Webster.

'He sure does,' Webster said neutrally, while not meeting Cassidy's eye, making Cassidy get up and stand before him.

'So you're claiming this is nothing like what happened to Hamilton?'

'It isn't. Hamilton was in a cell with two other prisoners, but this one was on his own.'

Cassidy waited for Webster to say more and perhaps offer a clue as to what he was hiding, but the jailer said nothing. To prolong his discomfort Cassidy returned to the body and moved around it as he examined the scene.

The pose of the body and the situation did look similar to last week's incident, and Webster was acting in the same cautious manner as he had shown before, too.

'I guess none of the other inmates saw anything either.'

'The cells are separated by walls. I wouldn't expect them to see or hear anything, so I didn't find out what had happened until I brought Ossie his breakfast.' Webster shrugged. 'At least I won't have to waste more food on this killer.'

Webster offered a smile that Cassidy didn't return. Instead, Cassidy moved out of the cell, but he stopped beside his jailer.

'Hamilton was a killer who'd have been of no use to anyone, but Ossie had a conscience and he might have helped me find the men who killed Klaude Stern and Barney Rose.' Cassidy waited for that information to sink in. 'Rest assured that I'll investigate both deaths thoroughly and I hope you're not found wanting.'

He waited until Webster gulped and then headed outside. As he stood on the boardwalk gathering his breath, a stage trundled by. When he noted that this one would have come from Prudence, he hurried on.

The stage stopped outside the Shaw Hotel and one man alighted. He had no luggage and even though the stage normally stopped for an hour before moving on to Carmon, it moved off immediately.

The man stepped out on to the hardpan to watch the stage leave. Despite the swirling dust, he stood with his legs planted wide apart, a light breeze rustling his long coat.

Cassidy walked up behind him meaning to ask if there was a reason for the driver leaving quickly, but the man turned to consider him. His piercing blue eyes were lively as if something about the situation had amused him.

'You must be Sheriff Cassidy Yates,' he said, in a calm and educated voice.

'I must be,' Cassidy said, refusing to ask for the man's name and confirm who he thought he was.

The man chuckled, perhaps because of his failure to ask the obvious question.

'We haven't met before, but I know plenty of folk here. Perhaps once I've booked a room, I may renew some old acquaintances.'

With that, the man turned to the hotel.

'Horace Franklyn went into town,' Volney Atwell said when he returned to the hollow. 'Now Laidley Rose is just sitting there on Horace's porch like he owns the place.'

'I guess he must be feeling confident we won't find him here,' Renard Icke said.

Renard patted Volney's shoulder and then moved off, but Volney didn't move.

'We need to talk about this first,' he said.

Renard turned round and stood over him.

'We don't. You've been asking too many questions since Ossie left us.'

'That's because he didn't have no choice about leaving. When you abandoned him in the post you said it was to teach him a lesson, but I gather he barely got out of there alive.'

'Then hopefully he's learnt his lesson.' Renard placed his hands on his hips, assuming that now that Volney had got his complaint off his chest, he'd join him, but he showed no inclination to move. 'But it looks as if you need to learn a few lessons.'

Volney clambered out of the hollow and he didn't speak until he faced him.

'I've not seen so much as a cent yet. I just have your word that this will be worth it, but since you left Ossie in the burning post, your word don't mean much to me.'

'I could tell you what you'll get out of this, but all your whining has probably alerted Laidley.'

Volney winced and with a nod he accepted he had been talking loudly. They moved on through the moonlit scrub, and when they reached the clear area before Horace's house, Renard's worst fears materialized.

Laidley was no longer on the porch.

He slapped Volney's chest backhanded and Volney returned a frown acknowledging he'd erred by questioning him.

'He might have gone back to hiding in the barn,' Volney whispered.

Renard turned to the barn, not relishing the thought of bursting into the dark interior in search of their target, when a loud voice spoke up behind them.

'He might,' the man said.

Renard assumed Laidley had spoken and he tensed.

'What do you want with us, Laidley?' he asked.

'I could ask you the same question.' Laidley

waited for an answer neither man could provide before continuing. 'I assume you're the men who burned down my brother's place.'

'I guess there's no point in denying that.'

Laidley grunted in anger. 'Then you need to know that Ossie didn't suffer his imprisonment for long. He was found dead in his cell this morning. As it seems that prisoners don't last long in the new jailhouse, you'll be pleased you won't have to end up there.'

This was news to both men and they glanced at each other in surprise. Then they both narrowed their eyes as they made an unspoken decision before they ducked down and sped away.

Laidley must have been aware of their likely intent as two rapid gunshots blasted, both shots slicing into the ground at their heels. With Volney in the lead they skirted round the edge of the clear area and headed towards the house.

When they reached the corner of the porch they hunkered down and turned around. They both loosed off shots at the place where Laidley had been, even though Renard doubted he'd still be there.

Sure enough, a gunshot whistled into the corner post inches from Renard's hand, coming from a spot only a dozen yards away. Laidley must have kept pace with them and taken up a new position where he couldn't be seen.

Volney fired wildly into the scrub, but when a

returning shot clipped the brim of his hat he cringed down and then scurried around the back of the house. Renard reckoned he had the right idea and he hurried after him.

It was darker behind the house and they moved on quickly across the bare ground. Only when they were a hundred yards from the house did the thought that they'd left their horses in the other direction make Renard come to a halt.

Volney must have had the same thought as he slowed, too, and the two men turned to look back at the house, which presented a darker shape against the night sky while all else was still.

'He's out there somewhere,' Volney said, his comment making Renard slap his hat to the ground in frustration.

'Then that's his mistake. I run from no man.'

'You've been doing plenty of running tonight and I reckon we should keep on running, or what happened to Ossie could happen to us.'

Renard nodded. 'It sounds as if Ossie didn't get a chance to talk about us, which is unfortunate for you.'

'Why?'

Renard raised his gun and glanced around as if looking for Laidley, making Volney follow his gaze. Then he lowered the gun and shot Volney in the leg.

Volney toppled over, clutching his leg, his screech echoing in the night. Renard dropped to one knee and dragged Volney's gun from his limp fingers.

As he hurled the gun into the night, Volney screeched again in pain. Laidley couldn't fail to have heard him and he'd be here within moments, but Renard still stood over the writhing man.

'Remember me,' he said. Then he shot Volney in the other leg.

CHAPTER 5

'So Renard Icke had good cause to be loitering around near your house,' Cassidy said, when he joined Horace Franklyn in Taylor's surgery.

Horace nodded. 'I searched around and found signs that someone had been sleeping in my barn recently. I'd guess that was Laidley Rose.'

Taylor had already removed two bullets from the wounded man and he was currently checking that Volney was fit enough to be questioned. Of Renard and Laidley, there was no sign.

'Hopefully Laidley will have moved on, so Renard won't trouble you again.' Cassidy patted Horace's shoulder and lowered his voice. 'But you need to know something: a man arrived on the stage from Prudence earlier. He booked into the Shaw Hotel and he was acting oddly.'

Horace flinched and put a hand to the wall to steady himself.

' "The law's delay. The insolence of office and the

spurns that patient merit of the unworthy takes".'
Horace pushed away from the wall and stood tall.
'I'll get Tormond to confirm who he is.'

While Cassidy searched for comforting words,
they stood in silence, but when Taylor came out of
the surgery Horace turned away. He picked up the
case containing his electrical contraption from a
table and patted the side as if that gave him
comfort, and then moved on.

'Keep the questions brief,' Taylor said, eyeing the
departing Horace with concern, suggesting he'd
overheard some of their exchange, 'but that should
be no problem. Volney's not like Ossie. He wants to
tell you everything.'

Cassidy nodded and headed inside to find that
Taylor had been right. The moment he stood
before Volney's bed he started explaining.

'Renard Icke got hired in Prudence to kill these
two men,' Volney said, the words running together
as he rushed to get them out. 'He never said what
they'd done wrong, but Ossie shot up the first one
no trouble, no trouble at all.'

'I saw that, so who hired Renard?'

'Renard dealt with him. Me and Ossie never saw
him, but Renard said he paid well.'

'Did Renard mention someone called Sykes
Caine?'

'No.'

'So how did you work out where Laidley was
hiding out?'

'Renard had a hunch where he'd be, but after he left Ossie and Barney in the post, we argued.'

'Because Renard killed Barney?'

'I didn't see him do it, but Renard sure shot me.' Volney gestured at his bandaged and immobile legs. 'Whatever help you need to get him, I'll provide it.'

'I'm obliged and if you're co-operative, it'll help you, provided you survive in our jailhouse for longer than Hamilton Davenport and Ossie Byers did.'

Volney winced. Then, with his story told, he flopped back on his bed.

Cassidy judged that he'd heard the truth, so he didn't pester Volney with more questions. As it was now too dark to pick up Renard's trail, he resolved to start the search in the morning.

Bearing in mind Ossie's fate and Volney's immobile state, he checked that Taylor wouldn't mind looking after Volney for a couple of days. Then he retired for the night.

In the morning, a few minutes after he opened up the law office Hearst joined him. While they planned their search and waited for Marcel to arrive, they both enjoyed coffees.

'I had a word with Marcel last night,' Hearst said, when it became clear the new deputy wouldn't join them, 'but he didn't accept my view. You ordered him to follow Renard and he won't rest until he finds him.'

'I gave him an order to follow the gunmen's trail,

not to follow Renard to the ends of the earth.'

'But you never told him to stop.' Hearst laughed. 'He's just being enthusiastic.'

'The problem with being enthusiastic is that he probably doesn't know that he's chasing after just the one man now.'

Hearst nodded. 'The bigger problem is that despite his efforts, he hasn't got close to Renard and he wasn't able to stop him trying to shoot up Laidley.'

Cassidy nodded. Then, when they'd finished their coffee, the two lawmen headed out of town.

They started their search at Horace's house where they found tracks heading away. As they followed them to the north and Spinner's Gulch, Hearst updated Cassidy on what he'd found in the records about Sykes Caine, which didn't amount to much.

Tormond hadn't kept extensive records and the little there was about Sykes provided no connection with Renard Icke, or any of the men at the heart of the current situation.

One of the few people who had been in town when Sykes had last been around was Laidley, but any hope that Laidley might help them died when they finally caught up with Marcel. The deputy was standing at the entrance to Spinner's Gulch and at his feet was a body that when they got closer turned out to be Laidley's.

They dismounted and joined Marcel.

'I presume this is the missing man?' Marcel said.

'It is,' Cassidy said, kneeling down beside the body. He considered the numerous bullet holes in Laidley's chest. 'He looks like he's been dead for several hours.'

As Marcel nodded, Cassidy noted that Hearst was looking perplexed. He joined the deputy and found him standing over two words etched out in the ground.

'I noticed that,' Marcel said. 'I wondered if Laidley had tried to say something before he died, but I don't reckon he'd have been strong enough to do that.'

'How like,' Cassidy said, noting the etched-out words. 'I guess this proves the previous message was important.'

'That's all it proves,' Hearst said. 'It don't make no sense.'

'The words aren't important. Sykes Caine left cryptic messages beside bullet-ridden bodies, and this proves he's involved with Renard.'

Hearst frowned. 'Then it's time we had a word with Sykes.'

'I promised Horace I'd give him time to talk with Tormond and they'd find out if the man in the Shaw Hotel is in fact Sykes. So that gives us time to follow Renard.' Cassidy moved over to Marcel and slapped his shoulder. 'Before we do that, you and I need to talk about what I expect from my deputies.'

'We can do that while following the trail,' Marcel

said. 'It's several hours old already, so we need to hurry.'

'We don't, because me and Hearst will follow Renard's trail while you return to town.' Cassidy pointed over Marcel's shoulder. 'A lawman's duties don't all involve gunfights and tracking outlaws. I want you to become familiar with Monotony. So patrol around and get to know its townsfolk while letting them see that a new lawman is in town.'

'If that's your order, I'll do it, but I can make my presence known any time. Renard's a slippery varmint and we need to find him.'

'We do, but you need to accept there could be another reason why an effective tracker like you hasn't found him.' When Marcel furrowed his brow, Cassidy turned to Hearst. 'Tell him, Hearst.'

'You've been riding around for days and you haven't got close to Renard,' Hearst said. 'That suggests that, like Laidley, he has a place to hole up. We know the area and where people hide out.'

'So,' Cassidy said, 'unless you know this area better than you've let on, you should return to town.'

Marcel sighed. 'I'll return to town.'

Cassidy and Hearst both nodded to him and so by the time the lawmen had mounted up, Marcel looked content with his new order.

'He's a bit like you were when I first appointed you,' Cassidy said as he and Hearst rode into Spinner's Gulch.

'That's odd,' Hearst said. 'I'd heard he's a bit like you were when you first became a lawman.'

Cassidy laughed before they turned their attention to the serious matter of finding Renard. As it turned out, they had no more luck than Marcel had and they failed to pick up Renard's trail or find any signs of recent activity at the usual hideouts.

The sun was setting when they turned back to town.

'It's looking as if with his task complete, Renard might have fled,' Cassidy said.

'Either that, or we were nearly right,' Hearst said. 'He's found somewhere to hole up, but in town rather than out of it.'

Cassidy nodded. 'Renard found his targets readily, which suggests he had help, so I'll question Volney again and find out just how disloyal he's prepared to be.'

With that thought cheering both men, they rode on, but when they approached town, their good mood ended. Raised voices were sounding and a commotion was in progress.

When they reached the main drag, they saw that it was centred around the Shaw Hotel. Dozens of people had gathered and many of them carried torches while the rest were shaking fists above their heads.

'The news about Sykes Caine must have got out,' Hearst said.

'At least we now know it is him,' Cassidy said with

a rueful smile. 'Hopefully we can get to him before this mob lynches him or burns down the hotel.'

They left their horses at the law office and hurried down the main drag. Once they reached the back of the crowd, they struggled to get anyone's attention as all eyes were on the hotel, even though there was nothing to see.

People had congregated around the entrance and they were straining to move forward, giving the impression that so many people were inside it was hard for anyone to advance. Tormond Quincy was standing on the periphery and he worked his way round the crowd to join them.

'I'm sorry,' he said. 'I tried to talk them down, but nobody would listen to a former lawman.'

'This situation isn't your fault and dealing with it isn't your responsibility either, but I assume this means the man in the hotel is Sykes?'

'When I tried to see him he wouldn't come to the door, but when he booked in he didn't give a name and that was good enough for Horace.'

'Where is Horace?'

'He's leading the mob!' Tormond shook his head sadly. 'After I failed to see Sykes, Horace said he'd try next, but he wanted a few hours to compose himself. As it turned out, he did all his thinking in the Two Bit saloon.'

'Horace never normally drinks liquor.'

'Which is a good job because he's a bad drunk-ard. He regaled the customers with tales of what

Sykes had done and by the time I arrived, he'd got everyone worked up. You can see the result.'

Cassidy nodded and then looked around.

'Where's Marcel Cartwright? I told him to make his presence known around town.'

Tormond furrowed his brow. 'I've yet to meet your new deputy.'

Cassidy sighed. 'Stay back and I'll see if I can make these people listen to a current lawman.'

With that, Cassidy and Hearst split up and moved around either side of the block of people. Everyone was so tightly packed together that Hearst soon disappeared from view.

When Cassidy reached the hotel wall, he wended his way into the throng. At first he made progress as the people ahead of him noted his presence with shamefaced looks. Then they moved aside while not catching his eye, but the closer he got to the door, the harder it became to make headway.

Before long he had to resort to slapping a hand on the shoulders of the person blocking his path and moving him aside. As that person could move only by shoving another person away, his action added to the consternation.

Soon people started shoving back and Cassidy found himself being buffeted along with no control of his direction. With his shoulders hunched from the people pressing up close on either side he concentrated on keeping his head high to see over the crowd and to his relief he saw that he was being moved to the door.

The pressure on either side grew until in a surge of motion he was squeezed through the doorway. He stumbled into the line of people before him, but to his relief there was slightly more space inside with everyone spreading out into the side rooms.

The stairs were ahead and everyone was facing them. The hotel owner, Stanley Shaw, was standing on solitary guard halfway up and he was remonstrating with Horace, who stood on the bottom step.

Their argument was clearly reaching a conclusion as Stanley was waving his arms angrily and Horace was shouting, his words indistinct and not carrying over the noise of the mob.

Then someone jostled Horace, making him stumble forward and go down on his knees two steps up. This encouraged a ripple of people to edge forward while Stanley backed away.

Cassidy reckoned that within moments the crowd would charge up the stairs and so he drew his gun and fired into the ceiling. The noise created sudden silence and the people ahead swirled round to face him.

While he had everyone's attention, Cassidy fired a second time and to his left Hearst matched his action with a gunshot into the ceiling.

'I apologize to Stanley for damaging his roof,' Cassidy called in the now quiet hotel, 'but you folks will all leave now.'

While still holding his gun high, Cassidy gestured

at the door. Several people nearby did as he'd asked and turned away, but with all the people between them and the door, it wasn't easy for anyone to move.

For several moments the people could only edge from side to side, but then from the stairs Horace cried out, ' "And now I'll do it! And so he goes to heaven. And so am I revenged." '

Then he hurried up the stairs with several men following him.

Stanley blocked his path, so Horace barged him aside and moved on. Stanley righted himself and tried to follow, but he was dragged back.

Within moments Horace led a straggling line of five men beyond the top of the stairs and then from view. Cassidy was relieved that nobody else moved to follow him and ran as fast as he was able to the stairs, reaching them at the same time as Hearst.

They collected Stanley and then hurried on. At the top of the stairs, Cassidy gave the mob below a warning gesture not to follow them and then ordered Hearst to stay there and ensure they disbanded.

He and Stanley moved on down the corridor to find that Horace had yet to gain access to Sykes's room. He was trying to shove the door open with his shoulder, but he wasn't making progress, suggesting Sykes had barricaded himself in.

When Horace stopped to rub his shoulder, two men took over. With a firm shove, they made the door edge open for a fraction, but then Cassidy reached them.

'This is over, Horace,' he said. 'I know what you think about Sykes, but you have no right to lead a mob here.'

'When Sykes came out of jail I'd have left him alone,' Horace said, 'but when he chose to come back here he brought this on himself.'

Cassidy moved forward as the door was knocked open for another few inches. He beckoned the two men who were barging into the door to back away.

'You're right,' he said, speaking loudly so he could be heard inside the room. 'Sykes made a big mistake, but I'm the law and it's my duty to protect everyone in town.'

'I know you're in a difficult situation, but you can't protect one man from a whole town. It'd be better for everyone if he just left on his own volition.'

With Horace talking sense and offering Sykes a way out, Cassidy hammered a fist on the door.

'You'll have heard that, Sykes. I'll protect you as best as I'm able, but pretty much everyone in town wants to tear you to pieces. Horace has offered you the only long-term solution. Move on.'

He waited and presently scraping sounded behind the door as Sykes moved furniture aside. Then the door swung open to reveal the object of everyone's ire.

'I have no intention of leaving,' the man said,

'until I've completed my business here.'

He smiled at Cassidy and then moved into the corridor to face Horace, who glowered with his posture tensing, making Cassidy think that despite his warnings he'd attack him. Then Horace's shoulders slumped and he lowered his head.

'That's not Sykes,' he murmured, his voice barely audible.

'He's not Sykes Caine?' Cassidy intoned, aghast. 'A near riot breaks out and it turns out that he's not Sykes!'

With Horace silent Stanley moved forward.

'I tried to tell Horace that every man has a right to his privacy,' Stanley said, 'and that didn't necessarily mean this man was Sykes Caine, but he wouldn't listen to me. At least he's seen the truth for himself.'

For long moments everyone stood in stunned silence until a door opened further down the corridor, breaking everyone out of their reverie. His deputy Marcel came out into the corridor and considered the gathered people with his arms folded.

Cassidy's presence didn't appear to perturb him as he fixed his gaze on Horace's back. With the crisis averted, Cassidy welcomed the thought of working off his anger on his deputy for failing to carry out his duty and he gestured at him to join them.

Marcel's footfalls caught Horace's attention and he turned around. Horace flinched before stumbling backwards a pace.

'The man in the hotel room might not be Sykes Caine,' Horace said. He pointed at Marcel. 'But that man sure is!'

CHAPTER 6

'So you're Sykes Caine,' Cassidy said, when he had closed the law-office door, 'not Marcel Cartwright?'

The new deputy shrugged. 'I didn't think you'd welcome me if I'd provided my real name.'

Back in the hotel Horace had been too shocked to act and the mob was dispersing, so Cassidy had got Sykes to the law office without incident. He'd last seen Horace being directed to the Two Bit saloon by Tormond, and Cassidy hoped Tormond could talk sense into him or the quiet time wouldn't last for long.

'What did you hope to gain out of the deception?'

'I hoped you'd get to know me rather than my reputation, and I reckon I was doing well.'

'At the start you did, then you were less effective. But I can see now that you were hamstrung by the fact you couldn't show your face in town.'

Sykes nodded. 'Now that there's no point in

hiding, I can play a full part in tracking down Renard Icke.'

Cassidy stared at Sykes in surprise, but when he returned his gaze he moved across the office and leaned back against his desk. Hearst matched his action while sporting an equally bemused look.

'You still expect to be my deputy?' Cassidy murmured, when he finally found his voice.

'Of course,' Sykes said with a light tone, as if the thought of dismissal had never entered his mind.

'You've spent ten years in jail for raiding a bank and from what I've heard that's just the start of your crimes.'

'I wouldn't expect a lawman to believe everything he hears.'

'I don't, so I assume you're going to claim you were wrongly convicted.'

'I've never done nothing wrong. I didn't raid no bank and I sure didn't kill anyone. Whether you want me as your deputy or not, I intend to prove my innocence, but I'd prefer it if I had the backing of the current sheriff of Monotony.'

Cassidy tipped back his hat. As any support he might provide would imply a criticism of a previous sheriff and a trusted friend, he beckoned Hearst to join him in leaving the office.

'Stay here while I talk to Hearst,' he said.

Hearst dallied to consider Sykes with disdain before, with a shake of his head, he followed Cassidy outside. They leaned back against the wall looking down the road towards the Shaw Hotel where everyone had now dispersed.

'That sure is some story,' Hearst said after a while. 'It sounds to me as if Sykes is just as devious as they say he is.'

'I asked you out here to hear your opinion on whether I should let him continue being my deputy, but I guess that answers my question.'

Hearst swung round to face him. 'You're not seriously considering doing that, are you?'

'He claims to be innocent, and he did help us out of a difficult situation when Renard ambushed Klaude Stern.'

'If we continue working with him, he'll get us into plenty of difficult situations. We might as well walk around with targets on our backs.'

'We're lawmen: we're used to that.'

'You are seriously considering this!' Hearst waved his arms as he struggled to find the right words to express his shock. 'Nobody will understand, especially Horace and Tormond. You'll lose the respect of the townsfolk along with every friend you have.'

'Except for one, I hope.'

Hearst sighed and looked aloft as he avoided the question.

'This is your decision, but even if giving Sykes the benefit of the doubt is the right thing to do, don't do it.'

Cassidy nodded, but he still took another minute before he went in and faced Sykes. With Hearst looking at him with concern, he stayed silent for another minute and appraised Sykes, who met his gaze levelly.

'You get one chance,' Cassidy said, his declaration making Sykes nod and Hearst draw in his breath sharply.

'Obliged,' Sykes said.

'You won't be so grateful once you face what's coming to you. Plenty of people hate you, or have been told they should hate you. You'll have to deal with that and you'll do it with words, not bullets.'

'I understand.'

'You'll also have to prove yourself by being a model deputy. Make one mistake and it'll be your last, so learn from the best by following Hearst.'

Cassidy glanced at Hearst, but he didn't welcome the praise as he stood with hunched shoulders, still glaring at Sykes.

'I'll start by finishing what I started,' Sykes said. 'I know how we can now complete our current investigation.'

'Does that mean you have an idea about where we can find Renard Icke?'

Sykes nodded, making Hearst snort.

'That's probably because he's in league with him,' Hearst said under his breath.

'While everyone was wondering if the newcomer to town was me,' Sykes said, his low tone showing he had heard Hearst, 'I was finding out who he really is.'

61

'And who is he?'

'He's Neal Davenport. I assume he's Hamilton Davenport's brother.'

'How did you find that out?' Hearst snapped.

'By being a model deputy.' Sykes turned to Hearst for the first time. 'Perhaps you could learn something by following me.'

'Why you . . .' Hearst muttered while advancing on Sykes, forcing Cassidy to step between them.

'That's enough,' he said. 'You two will find a way to work together.'

'I was working just fine without him,' Hearst said.

Cassidy waited for Sykes to retort, but when he said nothing, he pointed at each man in turn.

'Hearst, you'll give Sykes a chance to prove himself; Sykes, you'll prove to Hearst that you're worth that chance.'

Hearst backed away while shaking his head, but he said nothing more.

'I reckon I can do that,' Sykes said. 'Neal arrived with no luggage, but he didn't need any. The only time he ventured out of his room, he bought a new set of clothes. I figure that means he's a wealthy man.'

Cassidy nodded. 'A wealthy man in Prudence hired Renard Icke to kill Klaude and Laidley, and that would describe Neal. As he's come here, he probably hasn't paid Renard off yet.'

'So we just have to watch Neal and he'll lead us to Renard.'

Cassidy turned to Hearst, who acknowledged this made sense with a curt nod. With that being the extent of the understanding he expected to get from his two deputies that night, Cassidy turned to the door.

He stopped in the doorway. 'I'll leave you two to work out between you how you'll keep watch on Neal.'

Before either man could complain, Cassidy headed outside. He stood on the boardwalk listening to the stony silence inside the office and he allowed himself a smile before he dealt with his other, equally unwelcome task.

As it turned out the atmosphere in the Two Bit saloon was as tense and as silent as in the law office. Unlike most nights, the saloon was only half full, as most of the people who had descended on the hotel had returned to their homes.

Those who had come here sat in small, silent groups. Cassidy quickly found Horace and Tormond sitting in the corner. Tormond was nursing a coffee mug while Horace was clutching his case to his chest and rocking back and forth.

'Tormond saw you escorting Sykes to the law office,' Horace said when Cassidy sat down at their table. 'I presume you've dealt with him.'

'In a way,' Cassidy said. He leaned back in his chair giving both men time to relax and get a hint of what he'd done before he explained.

'So what have you done?' Tormond said, eyeing

Cassidy with concern.

Cassidy sighed. 'I appointed Sykes as my deputy before I found out who he really is. Apart from giving a false name, he's done nothing to make me give him an ultimatum, yet.'

'He killed Horace's daughter and two other men,' Tormond whispered. 'If that isn't enough, what is?'

'My duty is to deal with everyone fairly and sometimes that calls for me to—'

Horace snarled and then got up so quickly he toppled his chair and made the table rattle back and forth several times before it stilled. His action ensured that everyone in the saloon turned to watch him.

'When your duty calls for you to annoy good men, your supporters, your friends,' he said, 'then it's time to think again about that duty.'

With everyone watching them, Cassidy stood up, giving him time to choose his words carefully.

'You're speaking out of anger and if I were you, I'd punch me from here to the bar, but when you've got over that anger, I'm sure you'll respect that I haven't taken anyone's side.'

'Respect is earned, and right now you're not worth a bent dime.'

'In which case I'll make you the same promise I made Sykes. The moment he steps out of line, fails in his duty, or shows any sign of behaving like the man you reckon he is, I'll run him out of town so fast his boots will catch fire.'

Horace's eyes flared and he bunched a fist and shook it at Cassidy.

' "He has my dying voice. So tell him with the occurrents, more and less, which have solicited. The rest is silence." '

Then, seemingly needing a gesture to show his anger, Horace swung his case at Tormond's coffee mug and swept it to the floor. Then he turned on his heel and walked to the door.

Cassidy watched him leave and then sat. Tormond didn't turn to Cassidy until the saloon folk returned to their own business.

'Was that a threat?' Cassidy asked.

'I often don't understand Horace,' Tormond said, 'but this time I reckon he was telling you that he won't be speaking to you again.'

'Are you going to tell me I've done wrong, too?'

'I don't need to. You know you did wrong, because unfortunately, sometimes doing the right thing is wrong.'

Cassidy smiled. 'Hearst said something along the same lines.'

'But it didn't change your mind.' Tormond provided a tense smile. 'I'm sure many people will respect that you faced a difficult situation and you made the tough decision, even if they don't agree with it.'

'I did what I thought was best for everyone. Sykes gets the second chance he wanted and with everyone watching him, he might take it. If he doesn't, long before I run him out of town, I'm sure someone will make him regret coming back.'

Tormond sighed. 'He won't take that chance.'

'How can you be so sure?'

'Because he didn't come back here to make amends, or to prove his innocence, or to find the man who killed Availia and the rest – or whatever it is he claimed that swayed you.'

'I ask again: how can you be so sure?'

'Because you aren't the first one to fall for Sykes's devious ways.' Tormond shuffled his chair closer. 'He was once my deputy, too.'

'I didn't know that,' Cassidy murmured.

Tormond met Cassidy's incredulous gaze and then nodded.

'Sykes was with me for only three weeks. He found the first two bodies and I suspected nothing, and even when he found Availia I didn't work out what he was doing. To this day I regret my actions. If I'd been a better lawman, she'd still be alive.'

'You can't know that.'

'I can't.' Tormond stood up. 'But I do know that unless you deal with Sykes right now, everything that happened to me ten years ago will happen to you.'

CHAPTER 7

'He doesn't look worried that he might have been followed,' Hearst said.

'Then you should stop looking worried,' Cassidy said.

'I'm not worried about Neal.'

Hearst glanced at Sykes and then returned to looking down at their target. Sykes didn't speak, but his tense posture showed that the friction between the deputies was affecting him.

Clearly, despite organizing themselves to watch Neal for the last two days, the two men had yet to find common ground.

On the first day after the near-riot, Neal Davenport had taken the wise precaution of staying in the hotel, but on the second day he had taken a stroll around town. When nobody had taken exception to him, he had gone to the stable.

Shortly afterwards he'd ridden off. He'd headed to Riker's Bend, a mound that created a curve in the river four miles out of town.

The three lawmen had followed him at a safe distance and when he'd moved behind the mound, they'd hurried on while staying out of view. They'd found that he'd stopped on the other side, so they'd clambered to the top to await developments.

So far, Neal had mooched around beside the water. He mainly looked upriver or towards the setting sun, suggesting that whoever he was waiting to meet would come from that direction and that this person was due shortly.

Sure enough, a lone rider approached. He was riding downriver at an unconcerned pace and when he came closer, Cassidy saw that the man matched the description Volney Atwell had given him of Renard Icke.

Neal swung round to face the newcomer. While Renard was still riding they started up a conversation keeping Renard's attention on him. Cassidy directed his deputies to move into position.

As Renard dismounted, they moved down the other side of the mound. At the bottom they separated so they would come out on either side of the two men and trap them in a pincer movement.

When both deputies disappeared from view, Cassidy edged down towards Neal and Renard. He walked doubled over, dodging from boulder to boulder, only bobbing up to check on them infrequently for fear of being seen.

As the last twenty yards of the slope provided no cover, he hunkered down. He couldn't see Sykes, but he glimpsed Hearst slipping into position to his right.

Cassidy's order was for them to wait until Neal paid Renard, presuming that was the reason they'd met up, as at this moment they ought to be distracted. Accordingly, when Neal reached into an inside pocket, he tensed, but Neal had merely been adjusting his jacket.

Then, to Cassidy's surprise, Renard withdrew a bundle from his pocket and waved it at Neal. No matter what the nature of this transaction, Hearst chose this moment to announce his presence.

'Don't move,' he called, as he stepped out into the open.

Both men whirled round to face him. They considered him before dashing for their horses.

They had barely taken their first steps when Sykes, from the other end of the mound, fired two rapid gunshots while shouting out a warning. The shots were high, but they were well aimed as they spooked the horses, which skittered away.

Cassidy also fired two rapid warning shots.

'You're surrounded,' he declared.

Hearst backed up his comment with a high shot. With the lawmen's gunfire and their shouted demands making it sound as if their numbers were greater than they were, the two men scrambled for cover. The best they could manage was to hunker down at the bottom of the slope.

They looked to either side and, on finding both Sykes and Hearst with guns aimed at them, hurried upwards. That direction took them towards Cassidy and so the two deputies stilled their fire.

They had covered half the distance towards Cassidy before Neal noticed where Cassidy was lying in wait. He drew his six-shooter and, with a foot planted on a rock, he swung the gun up, but before he could aim at him, Cassidy had already picked him out with his gun.

Cassidy shook his head and Neal glared at him as he weighed up his chances. Cassidy kept half an eye on Renard expecting him to react first, but to his surprise he turned on his heel and ran to the right along the slope.

Neal used the distraction to snap up his gun arm and he delivered a wild shot that clipped into the boulder two feet to Cassidy's side. He adjusted his aim, but before he could fire again, Cassidy fired, slicing a high shot into Neal's left shoulder that made him stumble backwards.

Neal righted himself while twisting and then with one hand pressed to his shoulder he followed Renard, who found cover twenty paces away between two boulders. Neal fired on the run, so Cassidy hammered lead at his heels and that encouraged him to keep moving.

Cassidy fired one last shot that clattered into one of the boulders and then Neal joined Renard in disappearing from view. Cassidy raised himself and confirmed there was nowhere for the two men to go on the other side of the boulders and that they were trapped.

He waved at Hearst and Sykes, pointing out where their targets had gone to ground, and the two deputies ran along the bottom of the slope. When they took up positions ten paces apart facing upslope, Cassidy reloaded and then went to stand on the other side of the boulders.

The lawmen could keep them pinned down, and to shoot at the lawmen, Renard and Neal would have to risk emerging. Unfortunately, with the light level dropping, the lawmen had to move in before the gunmen could enjoy the cover of darkness, and so, in a co-ordinated move, they closed in.

Cassidy was pleased to see his deputies working well together. With only a glance at each other and a couple of gestures they agreed that Hearst would clamber on to one of the boulders so he could look down while Sykes approached from the front.

Cassidy backed up Sykes by approaching from the front on the other side of the boulders. He trained his gun on a gap that looked as if it extended for only a few feet, but more of it became visible without either man appearing.

He glanced at Sykes, who shrugged, while Hearst reached the top of the boulder and peered forward before backing away and shaking his head. Cassidy reckoned this meant the men were lying on the ground and so he adjusted his aim before he moved forward again.

Sure enough, Sykes took one step and then

flinched backwards, but not before a gunshot tore out that sliced into the ground at his feet. When he moved forward again he aimed lower.

Another gunshot sounded, but Cassidy didn't see where it landed and that encouraged the three lawmen to move quickly. Hearst lowered himself and then moved forward to where, with only a short movement, he could look down on the gap while Sykes and Cassidy positioned themselves either side.

'You've got five seconds to give yourselves up,' Cassidy said, 'or we end this here.'

Cassidy didn't expect them to surrender and was beckoning Sykes to slip his gun arm into the gap and fire blindly, when, to his surprise, Renard spoke up.

'Then I'll have to give myself up.' He snorted a laugh. 'Neal's in no state to do anything.'

Cassidy glanced at Sykes, who mouthed that he thought this a trap. So he looked at Hearst, who darted his head forward before flinching back.

Hearst looked surprised and then smiled, which encouraged Cassidy to move in.

Renard was lying on his chest with his gun thrown aside while Neal lay on his back bleeding heavily, his wound being further into his chest than Cassidy had thought.

At Cassidy's prompting Sykes moved in and kicked Renard's gun further away before dragging him to his feet. With Renard under control, Cassidy examined Neal, but his eyes had already glazed and he was no longer breathing.

'You're under arrest, Renard,' Cassidy said, 'for killing Klaude Stern along with Barney and Laidley Rose.'

Renard shrugged, seemingly unconcerned by the accusation.

'Ossie Byers was our keen-eyed shooter and he killed Klaude,' he said. 'Barney was alive when I last saw him, and the only time I got close to Laidley he nearly shot me up.'

Cassidy provided a disbelieving shake of the head and then directed Sykes to escort their prisoner downslope. Then Cassidy waited for Hearst to join him.

Hearst nodded, acknowledging that Sykes had done well, although his furrowed brow suggested that he still didn't trust him.

'It looks as if we've brought this investigation to a successful end, then,' Hearst said, when he took hold of Neal's arms.

'In some ways we have,' Cassidy said, taking Neal's legs, 'but there's still too many loose threads for my liking.'

'You don't believe Renard's protestations of innocence, do you?'

Cassidy didn't reply until they were halfway down the slope where he stopped to get a better grip of the body. He looked back up at the scene of the gunfight and then at the place where they'd watched the two men.

'I can't put my finger on it,' he said, when they

resumed walking, 'but something about this doesn't seem right.'

'Neal Davenport blamed Klaude and Laidley for his brother's death, so he hired Renard to kill them, which he did, no matter what he now claims. When Neal died, Renard gave himself up. It seems clear cut to me.'

'Except you watched Neal and he still arranged this meeting.'

'Perhaps he arranged to pay Renard earlier.'

'Which is another odd thing. When you interrupted them, it looked to me as if Renard was planning to pay Neal!'

When they reached the bottom of the slope, Hearst shook his head.

'I didn't notice that.' He glanced at their prisoner. 'But either way, Renard sure is a double-crossing varmint. He left Ossie to die and shot up Volney.'

Cassidy and Hearst lowered the dead man to the ground.

'Which brings up the last worrying point: Renard probably did plenty wrong, but Barney and Laidley died in similar circumstances to the unexplained deaths here ten years ago.'

'And those unexplained murders happened when Sykes was last in town,' Hearst said with a significant glance at Sykes.

'Like I said, there's too many loose threads for my liking.'

CHAPTER 8

Despite Cassidy's concerns about whether he had understood everyone's motives and ended the investigation, over the next two days he failed to confirm his misgivings.

The bundle Renard had been about to give Neal did contain money, but Renard refused to explain himself and confirm that Neal had hired him in Prudence to kill Klaude and Laidley. Volney also offered no further useful information and so both men were now in the jailhouse.

Sykes couldn't offer any suggestions as to what Renard might be hiding, but he offered one potentially useful lead when he reported that he was sure he'd met Renard recently, but he couldn't remember when.

As he'd been out of jail for only a short time, Sykes was sure he'd recall more details, but Cassidy didn't give him time to think. Figuring that the more opportunities to prove himself Sykes had the quicker he would justify his second chance, he kept Sykes occupied constantly with duties.

Most of those errands took him out of town while he and Hearst spent their time in it. Cassidy didn't detect any sign of the recurrence of the trouble that had erupted at the Shaw Hotel, although on the other hand, as promised, Horace ignored him. He didn't come across Tormond.

So he couldn't help but smile broadly when, as he was locking up the law office for the evening, Tormond came to see him.

'You must be pleased with yourself,' Tormond said. 'You solved a perplexing case and I gather Sykes acquitted himself well.'

'It was his good work that led to Renard's arrest.'

'So as far as you're concerned, all your problems are over.'

'The problems a lawman faces are never over.'

'That's never been truer. As I warned you, your problems are only just beginning.'

Tormond raised a hand when Cassidy started to ask for an explanation and beckoned him to follow. As soon as Cassidy moved away from the office, he saw that a commotion had erupted and, as he'd feared, it was centred on the Shaw Hotel.

When he approached, he found that only a dozen people had gathered so far and they were looking down the alley beside the hotel. Tormond moved back so that Cassidy could take the lead and he saw that Hearst had reached the alley first and he was talking with Doc Taylor.

The deputy broke off from his discussion and beckoned Cassidy to go behind the hotel. His sombre expression told him what he would find before he reached the back.

A man lay on his side. His chest was blooded and, when Cassidy laid him on his back, he noted the numerous gunshot wounds.

'Who is he?' Cassidy asked, when Tormond joined him.

'Nobody's recognized him yet,' Tormond said, 'but that's not as important as the way he died. The three people who died ten years ago were all shot repeatedly.'

Cassidy frowned. 'I've heard no gunfire recently. This man must have been killed out of town and then dumped here.'

'Sykes has been out of town and he's staying in this hotel.'

Cassidy shook his head. 'Sykes has been on duty elsewhere today and, besides, Renard Icke is still the most likely man to have killed Barney and Laidley.'

'Renard wasn't in Monotony ten years ago and now he's in jail, so he couldn't have killed this man.'

'I agree. I can't help but think that someone is trying to make it look as if Sykes killed him.'

Tormond shrugged. 'Sometimes the more obvious solution is the right one.'

Cassidy didn't want to be seen arguing the case for Sykes too strongly, so he stood back and considered the scene. His gaze fell on markings on the ground and, when he moved closer, he saw that another message had been left.

The first message beside Barney Rose's body had been one word and the second one beside Laidley's body had added a second. This message added a third with each short word presented above the other to provide a neat block of letters.

'How like a,' Cassidy said. 'An extra word is added after each death, but I can't see that the message will ever make sense.'

'The only way it could ever make sense is if more people die.'

Cassidy gulped. 'Is this how it happened to you?'

'Like I said, I got rid of Sykes before he completed whatever he was trying to say.' Tormond sneered at him for the first time that Cassidy could remember. 'It's a pity for you, and for this man, that you didn't take my advice.'

'Are you still ignoring me?' Renard Icke asked. He didn't get a response and so he stood in the corner of his cell nearest the corridor and repeated his question.

'Yeah,' Volney Atwell muttered after a while, 'other than to tell you to go to hell.'

Renard laughed and moved away from the bars. He had been placed in a cell on his own. Volney had the cell next to his. A wall separated them, but Volney had been carried past his cell and, aside from snarling at him, he'd not acknowledged him.

Volney was also alone and so Renard had given him until nightfall to speak.

'How are your legs?'

'They don't work, thanks to you, but if I ever get a moment alone with you, I'll make sure you find out just how much pain I suffered.'

'I doubt you'll get that chance. From what the lawmen said, I'm too dangerous to mix with other prisoners.'

Volney snorted a rueful laugh. 'From what I've heard, being left on your own in this jailhouse is dangerous enough. So don't relax too much in there.'

'I won't. I'm exactly where I want to be.' Renard settled down on his cot with his hands behind his head. 'And so now it begins.'

CHAPTER 9

'I heard what happened,' Sykes said, when he arrived at the law office in the morning. 'I know what you're thinking.'

Cassidy poured Sykes some coffee and stood beside Hearst to consider him. He and Hearst hadn't discussed the matter, but Hearst's tense posture suggested he expected Cassidy would now take decisive action.

'I'm thinking,' Cassidy said, 'what were you doing yesterday?'

'You know what I was doing. I checked out that report of people acting suspiciously near Matt Daley's ranch. It happened a week ago and we couldn't see any sign of them. Matt wasn't pleased it took this long to check it out and so I came back.'

'And then?'

'It was late. I ate in the Shaw where I heard what had happened, so I stayed there.'

'So you assumed you'd be suspected, even

though you were out of town at the time.'

'I was out of town the last time, but that didn't stop some people blaming me.'

'Nobody in this office is blaming you this time, but I'm sure those with long memories will find similarities with the three people who died when you were last in town.'

Hearst straightened up, but Cassidy sipped from his mug and that encouraged Sykes to relax and drink his coffee.

'Then maybe you should begin the search for the culprit with one of those people. Someone from those days must be responsible.'

'So, I'm looking for a killer who waited ten years to kill again and that man is also a thief who stole once and then never stole again.'

Sykes slammed his coffee mug down on his desk, spilling half the contents as he lost his temper for the first time that Cassidy had seen.

'I did nothing wrong when I was last here and I sure never robbed the bank in Prudence.'

'So what did happen?'

Sykes must have noted Cassidy's level tone as he mopped up the spillage and then picked up his mug.

'I came back to find Sheriff Quincy ransacking my room. He wouldn't tell me what he was looking for, but, as it turned out, he found bills and legal documents in a case beneath my bed. Apparently they'd gone missing from the Prudence bank.'

'I can see how that would look bad for you. After all these years, I doubt you'll ever prove your innocence.'

'I doubt it, too. On my way here I visited Prudence, but I couldn't find anyone who even remembered the bank being raided. So I—' Sykes looked aloft with his eyes narrowed and then nodded.

'What have you just remembered?'

'I said I'd seen Renard Icke before and I've remembered where now. He was in a saloon in Prudence.'

'He was probably there to meet Neal Davenport. We should visit Prudence and check it out.'

Cassidy glanced at Hearst for an opinion, but he said nothing.

'I'm sure we won't learn anything we don't already know,' Sykes said.

'Perhaps we won't, but there's still plenty of loose threads in this case. I need to clarify Renard's activities and it'll let me find out more about this bank raid.' Cassidy gestured at the door for Sykes to leave first. 'And it'd help if you weren't seen around town for a few days.'

Sykes turned to the door, but Cassidy stayed where he was.

'See you in a few days,' Hearst said, when Sykes had left.

'You got nothing to say about this mission?'

'Nope.'

Cassidy snorted a laugh, although he hated hearing the dry tone Hearst used whenever he spoke to him now.

'You appear to have adopted a policy of not commenting on anything connected with Sykes.'

'I thought it was for the best, as you won't listen to anything I might say about him.'

Cassidy nodded. 'While I'm away, see what you can learn about this new dead man. Hopefully no more bodies will turn up while I'm gone.'

'They won't, while you're gone.' Hearst collected the coffee mugs as Cassidy headed to the door, but Hearst spoke up when he was in the doorway. 'Be careful.'

'I hope spending time with Sykes will make everything clearer. By the time I return I expect to know what's the right thing to do, even if it's the wrong thing.'

With that, Cassidy moved on. The townsfolk were beginning to stir and so he and Sykes didn't dally before leaving town.

'I can't keep hiding,' Sykes said, when they were twenty miles out of town, 'but I'm obliged you're willing to check out my story.'

'I will, but it's yet to be proven whether it'll help you or not.'

Sykes sighed. 'I reckon the only thing that could help me is a body turning up while we're gone.'

'I wouldn't wish that to happen.' Cassidy frowned. 'But if it did, who would you suspect?'

'I'd prefer to keep my thoughts on that to myself.'

'You've had ten years to think about it, so you must have some ideas, and it's a journey of several days to Prudence and back.'

'Like I said, I'd prefer not to mention my suspicions.'

Sykes waited until Cassidy opened his mouth to argue and then pointed back along the trail. Cassidy turned in the saddle and noted that a rider was galloping after them and he would join them in another few minutes.

Cassidy narrowed his eyes and, to his surprise, he identified Tormond Quincy. He stopped to wait for him, but when he'd overcome his shock, he recalled Sykes's last words.

'Are you saying you don't want to mention your suspicions when the man who arrested you is about to join us? Or are you saying you suspect Tormond?'

'You wouldn't believe either answer, but all I'm saying is: I didn't kill anyone and I didn't know that the stolen money was in my room.'

Cassidy didn't reply as he waited for Tormond.

'I heard you'd left town,' Tormond said when he drew up. 'I told Hearst I'd let you know what I've found out. The dead man was Gerald Norton.'

'The name means nothing to me,' Cassidy said.

'It means plenty to me, although I've never met him before. He was once a notorious bandit, but I haven't heard about him for years.'

'And this notorious bandit just happens to turn up dead behind the Shaw Hotel.'

'Which is sure to anger many. He had plenty of friends and the word is out that Sykes killed him.'

'Obliged for that,' Sykes murmured.

Tormond hunched forward in the saddle, but with a bunched jaw he clearly forced down the retort that came to mind and addressed Cassidy.

'I don't care none what happens to the man riding with you, but if Norton's friends come after him, you could be in trouble.' Tormond moved his horse on to slip between them. 'So I thought I'd ride along with you awhile.'

In the ten years since Tormond had last been a lawman, he had never once made such an offer. Even if he had, Cassidy would have refused it, but bearing in mind his conversation with Sykes, he couldn't help but think that Tormond was worried what Sykes might reveal.

On the other hand, one of his reasons for under-taking this journey was to make Sykes uncomfortable and so perhaps uncover the truth, and Tormond's presence was sure to make him even more uneasy.

Cassidy nodded and so the three men moved on towards Spinner's Gulch. Despite Tormond's warning, the terrain was open enough for them not to take additional care, but when they reached the gulch, Cassidy moved on ahead.

Without incident they passed the place where

they'd found Laidley's body and then the scene of the recent ambush. When they reached the railroad bridge that marked the end of the gulch, he waited for the other two men to join him.

Then, in single file, they led their horses across the bridge. The river below was swollen and the roar of the water was so loud it made conversation hard, but Cassidy relaxed for the first time since Tormond had joined them.

He assumed that any trouble they might face would come from men following them out of town, but when they reached the end of the bridge splinters kicked from the end stanchion.

A gunshot blast sounded a moment later. That heralded the start of a sustained volley of lead that ripped across the bridge, sending shards flying from the posts and sparks from the rail tracks.

The gunfire was coming from ahead and they were exposed out on the bridge. So the three men abandoned their mounts and with their heads down they ran towards land.

When Cassidy reached the end stanchion, he hunkered down. He figured that if one of the shooters had hit the post, that man should be in his line of sight.

Sure enough, as Tormond and Sykes peeled away from the rail tracks and went left, one man bobbed his head up and took aim at them. He was thirty yards away on the left of the bridge and he'd been lying in a hollow.

Before he could fire, Cassidy ripped off a quick shot that skittered into the dirt five feet before the gunman. The gunshot made the gunman duck back down without firing. Even better, Tormond looked over his shoulder and saw him before he and Sykes scrambled over the lip of the gorge and lay down on their chests.

Tormond even got over his distaste of speaking to Sykes and pointed out where the man was. A few moments later two more men bobbed up twenty feet away from the first and one fired off a couple of wild shots at Tormond's position while the other's shot hit the stanchion.

As Cassidy took cover, he thought back to the start of the ambush. Although the gunfire had been fierce, he judged that it was likely that only these three men had been involved.

He gestured at Tormond and Sykes signifying that they should provide covering fire while he moved to a mound where he would be able to look down into the hollow. Both men nodded and so Cassidy edged out from behind the stanchion as he prepared to make his move.

The gunmen, though, had plans of their own and charged out from the hollow while firing. Tormond and Sykes dropped down while the gunmen's movement was so sudden that Cassidy took a moment to follow them with his gun.

The nearest gunman took advantage of his slowness and while running tore out a shot that whistled past Cassidy's shoulder making Cassidy dive on to his chest on the end of the bridge.

As a second shot flew over his head, he rolled once and came to rest behind the limited cover of the rail tracks. He took aim at the gunmen, picking out the central man who had shot at him, and fired.

His shot missed his intended target, but with the men appearing close together from his position, he caught the trailing gunman with a shot high in the arm. The blow made the man stumble, letting Cassidy dispatch him with a deadly shot that sliced into his neck.

The other two kept running while keeping their attentions on Sykes and Tormond, although after they took two more paces Cassidy could see that their target was Sykes.

Cassidy loosed off another shot, but the other corner stanchion blocked some of his view and the slug sliced into the ground several feet behind them. But he saw Tormond raise himself to be confronted by the sight of the two men looming over him.

Tormond fired into the stomach of the nearest man, making that man fold over, although the gunman's rapid pace made him stumble on until Sykes dispatched him with a second shot that made him tumble to the ground.

On the run, the third man reached Sykes, but with Sykes presenting a low profile, his shot hammered over his head, and when Sykes returned fire it flew wild.

Then the guntoter leapt at Sykes, grabbing his shoulders and carrying him down the slope with him. Cassidy jumped to his feet and ran forward to see them roll for several yards before they shuddered to a halt.

They were twenty feet away from the long drop down into the river and Cassidy reckoned if they struggled they could both start rolling again. The gunman must have noted this danger as he extricated himself from Sykes's arms.

The man had his back to Tormond and Tormond snapped up his gun arm to shoot him. From Tormond's position, Sykes was to the gunman's side and he had a clear view of the guntoter, but he didn't fire.

When Sykes moved groggily, the gunman thudded a punch into Sykes's stomach that sent him reeling, but he landed on an area where the slope was slight and he came to rest after only one roll.

As the gunman advanced on Sykes, Cassidy ran to the side of the bridge and took aim at him. As a poor shot would hit Sykes, he steadied his hand.

The gunman slapped two hands on Sykes's back, drew him up to a crouched position, and then moved to swing him towards the river.

Cassidy tightened his trigger finger, but he didn't need to fire as Tormond finally shot at the gunman. He hit him squarely in the back of the head, making him release Sykes and fall forward.

As he tumbled over and went plummeting down to the river, Sykes dropped down on to his chest and hugged the earth. For his part, Tormond stayed still with his gun aimed at the gunman's former position, and he was still there when Cassidy joined him.

'Don't say it,' Tormond muttered.

Cassidy nodded, and then held out a hand to help Tormond clamber back up on to flat ground, but he didn't move until Sykes stirred and looked up at him. He took Cassidy's hand and then moved on, leaving Cassidy to help Sykes back up.

By the time Sykes clambered over the lip of the slope, Tormond was kneeling beside one of the two dead gunmen.

'I'm glad you warned us we might be followed,' Cassidy said, 'but at least this now means you can head back to Monotony.'

'It doesn't,' Tormond said. He looked up and frowned. 'This man isn't one of the men I thought would be following you.'

CHAPTER 10

'So who were they?' Cassidy said, when they'd made camp for the night.

'The one I recognized was Elam Forrest,' Tormond said, while watching Sykes, who winced.

'I've never heard of him.'

'He's another name from the past. He associated with Yancy Dix, the first man that Sykes . . . the first body that turned up ten years ago. I'd guess he and the other men were waiting for Sykes to come out of jail.'

'At least we haven't seen the men who were friends of Gerald Norton. So hopefully that means our problems are over.'

'Or it could mean your problems are just beginning.'

Tormond waved an angry hand at Sykes, who spoke up for the first time in a while.

'If the associates of Yancy Dix took exception to me,' he said, 'it's likely that someone connected to the second man to die ten years ago, Peter Thornley, will come after me, too. Peter was even more trouble than Yancy was.'

Tormond snorted a rueful laugh. 'I might not be around the next time to save your hide.'

'I'm grateful you did it the once. That means a lot to me.'

'It shouldn't. For all you know I could have been aiming at you.'

'You weren't and that means you must doubt that I'm guilty, even if you won't admit it to me, Cassidy, or even yourself.'

Tormond turned to look into the flames. Cassidy gave both men a chance to speak again, but when they didn't he leaned forward.

'I haven't considered who the dead men were ten years ago as the records didn't include much detail, but it sounds as if the two men to die were outlaws, and so was Norton.'

Tormond shrugged. 'I don't reckon that's relevant. Availia was no outlaw and that didn't stop. . . .'

Tormond trailed off and then with a grunt he moved round the fire to put as much distance as he could between himself and Sykes.

'So first you acted when it mattered,' Sykes said. 'Now you can't bring yourself to repeat your accusation. Soon you'll be admitting I never robbed that bank.'

Tormond tensed, but he didn't reply. Cassidy raised a hand.

'That's enough, Sykes. We're sure to face enough danger from the gunslingers who want to kill you; it'd be best if we don't kill each other before they find you.'

'Except that's why we're going to Prudence, isn't it? I'm sure you've got contacts there who could find out what Renard's business was, and there has to be records about the bank raid, but that wouldn't let you spend time with me so you could figure me out. Tormond joining us is a bonus.'

Cassidy favoured Sykes with a smile.

'You're right that I hoped to learn more on the way to Prudence than I might find out when we got there, but that means you have an audience. So tell me your side of the story.'

Sykes leaned forward to poke the fire and then threw the stick in the flames. Tormond made a show of rolling over to put his back to them, but Cassidy could tell he was alert.

Sykes watched the stick until it caught fire and then faced Cassidy.

'A day after being sworn in as Tormond's deputy I found Yancy Dix's body. Tormond reckoned it was a fitting end after his exploits and he let me tie up the case. It was my first investigation and I was diligent, but I got nowhere. Then a second outlaw's body turned up. I was sure they were connected.'

'Because they were both killed elsewhere and then dumped outside town with multiple gunshot wounds?'

Sykes nodded. 'I was trying to work out what the messages beside the bodies meant when Availia's body turned up beside a new message.'

Sykes's voice broke and he coughed, making Cassidy nod.

'You knew her?'

'We were getting friendly. I reckoned she'd been killed as a warning to me because I was getting close to working out who was doing it, but I never got the chance after the money was found in my room.'

'And who did you suspect?'

Sykes's gaze darted to Tormond in an unconscious gesture before he shrugged.

'I suspected plenty of people, but I'd guess not many of them are left in town now.'

Cassidy nodded and completed the thought.

'But if people are being killed again in the same way, it should be possible to work it out.'

Although he tried not to, he glanced at Tormond, who still had his back turned, and when Cassidy looked back at Sykes, he was smiling.

The sign above the door of Prudence's bank offered the proud boast that it'd never been raided. Tormond didn't appear to notice it as he headed inside first and sought out an old friend, the teller, Luke Edwards.

After the turmoil of the first day of the journey, the rest of the trip to Prudence had been uneventful. They hadn't discussed past events again while

Sykes and Tormond had avoided each other as much as possible.

They'd seen no sign of anyone following them, but now that they were amongst people again, Cassidy wanted to deal with business quickly. So while he and Tormond checked out the bank, he let Sykes leave to find the saloon where he'd seen Renard.

Luke led them through to an office where they exchanged pleasantries before moving on to discuss the raid.

'I've not thought about that for years,' Luke said with a frown, 'and these days everything is different here. We've had no other trouble.'

Tormond nodded and then backed away, as if Luke had provided all the information Cassidy could want.

'I'm not worried about recent trouble,' Cassidy said. 'A man spent ten years in jail because of the last raid and I'd welcome more details.'

Luke sneered. 'I'd have given him longer. Then you wouldn't have to waste my time asking about it.'

Cassidy noted that Luke hadn't asked him why they were interested in what had happened. When he didn't reply, Luke glanced at Tormond, who tipped his hat and turned to the door.

Cassidy stayed and folded his arms. 'I'm sorry to waste your no doubt valuable time on such an old matter, but I've come a long way to talk to you. So how did the raid happen? Who else was involved?

How did the money get to Monotony?'

'That's a whole heap of questions.'

Cassidy waited, but when he didn't get a whole heap of answers, he glanced at Tormond, who was still loitering in the doorway.

'I reckon Luke is trying to tell you,' Tormond said, 'that this happened a long time ago. He was just a teller and he can't help you.'

'In my experience tellers know the most about raids,' Cassidy said, 'although whether they'll tell a lawman what they know is another matter.'

'I resent the inference,' Luke blustered. 'I didn't take no bribe to look the other way.'

Cassidy smiled. 'I meant that tellers are often threatened during a raid and afterwards they're too scared to talk.'

When Luke winced, Cassidy turned away. Tormond stayed to exchange a quiet word with Luke and then followed him out.

'I know what you're thinking,' Tormond said when he joined him outside. 'You shouldn't assume that the raiders got help from someone in the bank. This bank is one you can trust.'

'I'll do that.' Cassidy pointed at the sign above the door. 'Apparently it's never been raided. I can't help but wonder whether that statement might, in fact, be true.'

Wisely Tormond stayed quiet. Sykes emerged from the saloon and they joined him. He reported that he'd made progress and so for the next half-hour they followed him around town as he visited two more saloons, a store and a bath-house.

The information he gathered led him to Chester's hardware store. While Sykes questioned Chester, Cassidy roamed around the store so that he could avoid dwelling on the interview in the bank in which his failure to learn anything had told him everything he needed to know.

The raid ten years ago wasn't what it seemed and it may even have never happened, which left him with the problem of who had been involved in fabricating the story.

He struggled to think of anything he could say to Tormond and so he was pleased when the store's merchandise gave him an opportunity to chat. Facing the window was a table displaying Horace's contraption.

'Professor Polonius Ponting's Extraordinary Electrical Machine,' Cassidy said, reading the sign propped up behind an open case.

'I'd wondered where he got it from,' Tormond said.

Cassidy pointed at the endorsements that boasted the device would let the owner be at the forefront of a revolution that would change all their lives. It would also treat a variety of maladies that were beyond the understanding of doctors including ailments, not just of the body, but nervous complaints of the mind and failings of the soul.

'And I wondered where he got his explanation of

what the device would do.'

Tormond shrugged. 'You shouldn't be sceptical. He's found plenty of people who'll pay to have him use the machine on them. I can't say it's done them any good, but it's taking Horace's mind off his problems.'

Cassidy nodded, but then, with Sykes having got the information he wanted, Tormond turned away. Sykes was smiling, but unfortunately Chester had noticed what they had been looking at.

'Would you like a demonstration?' he asked, rubbing his hands with glee.

'No,' Cassidy said. 'I've already seen one before. Horace Franklyn in Monotony has one.'

'Indeed he does, and you'll be pleased to learn that you could afford one of your very own.'

Chester picked up one of the handles and waved it at Cassidy; Cassidy backed away.

'I wouldn't want to interfere in his business.'

'I'm sure you wouldn't,' Chester persisted. 'Horace's machine is a special one that he had specially built, but this is a cheaper model.'

Now that he'd mentioned it, Cassidy could see that the case Horace owned was larger. He looked the device over, wondering what else might be different, but Chester took his interest as a sign of a possible sale and he tapped the end of the handle against Cassidy's hand.

This device might have been smaller than Horace's, but it delivered a greater shock, making

Cassidy snatch back his hand. He rubbed his skin, finding he'd received a small burn, which made Chester look horrified as he saw any chance of a sale disappear.

He fussed over him, but Cassidy shooed him away and then joined Sykes and Tormond in leaving. Apparently, Sykes reported, Chester had given him the name of someone who had spent time with Renard when he'd been in town and so they visited the nearest saloon in search of this man.

He wasn't there so they moved on. By the time they were heading into the third saloon, Tormond was smiling at Cassidy, who was fingering his burn with irritation.

'It's hard to believe people can be fooled into buying contraptions like that one,' Cassidy said.

'People have always been conned by stories,' Tormond said, glaring at Sykes, who had just found someone to talk to at the bar. 'Just like you're being reeled in at the moment.'

'I know Sykes could be taking us around town until he gets a chance to run, but I'm giving him that chance because one chance is all he'll get.'

Tormond grunted under his breath as if he didn't approve of this plan and his mood didn't lighten when Sykes hurried over with a smile on his face.

'I've got the answer I was looking for,' he said, beckoning them to join him.

Sykes didn't explain until they reached the bar

where he directed Walter, the man he'd been conferring with, to tell his story.

'Like I told Sykes,' Walter said, 'I met Renard Icke at this bar and told him what he wanted to know.'

'Which was?' Cassidy said, as Sykes's smile widened in anticipation of the explanation.

'He was looking for Neal Davenport.'

Sykes nodded steadily, implying that this revelation should have amazed them, but Cassidy shrugged.

'I already knew Renard met someone in Prudence and I'd assumed that was Neal.'

'But we thought that Neal hired Renard,' Sykes said. 'We got it wrong: Renard hired Neal.'

Walter provided an affirmative grunt making Cassidy think back to what he'd seen at Riker's Bend. Back then, he'd been sure that Renard had been preparing to pay Neal.

'You must have got that wrong,' Tormond said, shaking his head. 'Neal sought out Renard because Neal's brother had been killed in Monotony's jailhouse and he wanted revenge.'

'He didn't,' Walter said, with a triumphant gleam in his eye. 'Renard sought out Neal because Renard's brother had been killed in Prudence's jailhouse and *he* wanted revenge.'

He looked around the surprised men while licking his lips. As they'd already divulged as much information as they'd received, Cassidy signified that they should move away.

Sykes stayed to slip Walter a couple of dollars before he joined them. He was still smiling with a look that said he still had more to tell.

'So if Renard's motivation was revenge and not money,' Cassidy said, 'why did he go after the two men who were with Hamilton Davenport when he died?'

'I don't know,' Sykes said, 'but I've learnt one other thing that might help to explain it. Webster Todd was the jailer in Prudence's jailhouse when Renard's brother was found dead in his cell. Nobody found the death suspicious, but then Webster moved on to Monotony.'

Cassidy winced. 'And since Webster came to Monotony to work as our jailer, two prisoners have died in the jailhouse.'

CHAPTER 11

It was late into the night when Webster Todd came for him.

Renard Icke was awake. With Volney in the next cell ignoring him and with nothing to occupy his mind he'd slept during the day, figuring that nothing would happen during daylight hours.

At night he had stayed quiet on his cot, hoping to look as if he were a prisoner biding his time. The scraping of a key in his cell door was the first sign that his caution and vigilance would pay off.

He breathed audibly, giving the impression that he was sleeping. Then he stirred with a subdued groan, as if he'd heard a noise but that it hadn't been loud enough to wake him, while using the movement to get into a position where he could get up quickly.

The creaking stopped, making him fear that he'd erred and frightened the jailer off, but then the cell door squeaked open. Lying beside the wall he was

in darkness and so he half-opened an eye and confirmed that what he'd heard was correct.

The door was open and the dark form of the
jailer stood two paces away looking down at him.
Webster was as still as a statue, clearly watching him
to confirm that he was in fact sleeping.

The long moments dragged on Renard's nerves,
making him struggle to appear relaxed when his
muscles were tensing with every heartbeat.

His reckless plan hinged on this moment.

While completing his bargain with Neal by tracking down the men Neal had thought responsible,
he had followed his own theory. He had needed to
get arrested and thrown in jail where he hoped that
whatever had happened to his brother would
happen to him, except unlike the others, he'd be
ready for it.

That meant he had to seize this opportunity, but
he had no weapon and he had no knowledge of
what to expect from Webster, other than the likely
result of failure.

Webster murmured to himself, seemingly making
a decision, and then swooped down on him. One
hand lunged for Renard's mouth to keep him silent
while the other hand moved to secure him around
the neck.

Neither hand closed on its intended target. With
Renard's senses heightened he reacted with enough
speed to avoid Webster's lunge and while Webster
floundered over the cot, he rose up quickly.

He gained his feet and then turned the tables on Webster by stepping up behind him and wrapping his left arm around his neck while with his right hand he gripped his jaw. Then he swung him round to mash his body up against the bars.

'One wrong move and I'll snap your neck,' Renard said in Webster's ear. He waited until Webster grunted an acknowledgement before continuing. 'I want answers: you'll provide them.'

'What do you want to know?' Webster asked with a shaking voice.

'Prisoners die in cells that you guard and I want to know why.'

'I'm not the only jailer here and I'm not the only person who sees the prisoners.'

'I know that and that's why I haven't killed you yet. So keep talking and you can keep living.'

'I haven't killed nobody.'

Renard waited for more, but Webster tensed, as if this declaration would satisfy him. Then distant footfalls sounded, showing what had provided Webster with more confidence.

'Are you saying that you've done nothing wrong,' Renard whispered, 'but this man has?'

Webster provided a sharp nod and so Renard listened to the footfalls. They were slow and deliberate, and the man stopped at the end of the corridor with a squeaking of his boots before he moved on.

He paced along the corridor, his boots now thudding followed by a click, as if he were tapping something against the bars. Renard and Volney were the only prisoners on this side of the jailhouse, but even so, Renard judged that people who arrived openly would attract less attention than those being secretive.

Renard edged forward hoping to see the newcomer and answer the question that had burned in his mind since Neal Davenport had told him his brother wasn't the only one to die in a jailhouse recently.

He didn't know what he'd face, but, as he prepared to keep Webster subdued and take on the newcomer, Webster took advantage of the distraction. He jerked his elbow backwards into Renard's stomach, making him grunt in pain.

The footfalls and tapping stopped and so angry now that his plans might unravel, Renard hurled Webster aside and made for the door. The blow had winded him more than he'd thought and he stumbled.

Feeling light-headed, he put a hand to the bars. He righted himself and made for the doorway, but he had yet to reach it when Webster leapt on his back.

Renard doubled over and swung round, sweeping Webster's feet from the floor, but Webster retaliated with a punch up into Renard's face. Webster couldn't get much force behind the blow, but it crunched into Renard's nose and the burst of pain made him stumble to one knee.

The moment Webster's feet landed on the floor, he grabbed Renard around the midriff, lifted him to his feet, and ran him at the door. Renard's forehead collided with the bars with a resounding clang that sent the door swinging into the wall before it rebounded and delivered a second, lighter blow to his shoulder.

Renard waved his arms weakly, trying to grab hold of Webster, but he couldn't reach him and Webster had no intention of relinquishing his advantage. He drew Renard upright and thudded a punch into his kidneys that made Renard double over.

Before he could recover, Webster hurled him at his cot, making him roll on to it and slam into the wall. He lay, his confused senses ensuring he was unable to fight back, but Webster didn't follow through with a further assault.

By the time Renard sat up, Webster had locked the cell door and moved out of view. With a groan Renard twisted round on his cot to face the bars, but Webster didn't come back into sight and neither could he see the newcomer.

He rubbed his forehead and, as his senses returned, he tried to accept that he'd ruined his one chance and now he'd probably never find out the truth. Then he heard voices nearby and he realized that Webster and his unknown accomplice hadn't left.

Renard rubbed his side and rolled his shoulders as he prepared himself for whatever they tried next.

Then he registered that the voices were in the cell next to his. Volney was speaking and his voice was low and pleading.

Webster replied and then a thud sounded, followed by scrambling noises. A clang resounded through the cell and then scraping sounds.

'Please, don't,' Volney murmured.

'The more you struggle, the more it'll hurt,' Webster said.

Silence reigned for several seconds. Then Volney screamed.

Any doubts about the intentions of Gerald Norton's friends fled when Cassidy rode back into Monotony.

Tormond pointed out the four men who were standing opposite the law office. Their slouched postures gave the impression they'd kept lookout since Cassidy had left town.

Worse, they weren't the only new faces in town. Two men were loitering outside the Two Bit saloon and they peeled away from the wall to follow them while Cassidy noticed other surly men watching their arrival.

None of these men glared at them with as much venom as Horace did when they passed him. Tormond stopped to talk to him. The two lawmen carried on to the law office and went inside.

'These new faces give you any trouble?' Cassidy asked Hearst.

'Not yet,' Hearst said with a glance at Sykes that

said he thought that would change now. 'But we've had plenty of other trouble.'

'At the jailhouse?'

'How did you know. . . ?' Hearst sighed. 'Volney Atwell was found dead in his cell this morning. Like the other prisoners it looked like an accident, but I'm glad you're back because it sounds like you might have an answer.'

Cassidy nodded. 'I do, and it's time we ended this situation.'

Cassidy indicated that Hearst should come with them and his stern expression ensured he didn't ask any questions. When they were outside, Cassidy noted that the men opposite the law office hadn't made a decisive move, but the other men who had watched them arrive had gathered on the edge of town, suggesting there were two groups.

Cassidy surmised that as they'd prevailed against the associates of Yancy Dix and one group knew Gerald Norton, the other group could want revenge for Peter Thornley's death.

'You sure have plenty of friends,' Hearst said, as the three men walked to the jailhouse.

'I'm amazed they all gathered so quickly,' Sykes said. 'It makes me wonder who told them I was here.'

Cassidy and Hearst both conceded this was a good point with grunts before they headed into the jailhouse. Three men were on duty and they were lounging around the office.

Webster Todd eyed him with concern. The other two jailers, Victor and Declan, had appeared sufficiently annoyed by the previous deaths to suggest that they weren't involved in Webster's activities.

'I gather someone else died while I was away,' Cassidy said.

'A prisoner who shot up another ex-prisoner died,' Webster said. 'It's how it goes with these people.'

'I agree, but this time it happened while I was visiting Prudence.' Cassidy waited until Webster winced and then caught Hearst's eye. 'You used to be the head jailer there, didn't you?'

Webster glanced at the door, and that was enough for Hearst to move in and grab him, even though Cassidy hadn't explained his suspicion. Victor and Declan offered no comment while backing away, giving further credence to Cassidy's assumption.

'I knew I'd get blamed for that one day,' Webster said when he found his voice. 'That's why I left Prudence.'

'Your reputation didn't follow you here, but the bodies did. Now you can enjoy being a prisoner. I hope Declan and Victor look after you better than you looked after your charges.'

Declan moved in and took control of Webster, who struggled before going meekly out of the room. Nobody spoke until a cell door slammed shut.

'That was progress,' Hearst said, 'but it doesn't

explain everything that's been happening.'

'I know,' Cassidy said. He turned to Victor. 'In which case you have a second man to escort to a cell.'

'When do you hope to bring him in?' Victor asked.

'He's already here.'

Everyone was silent until Sykes grunted in anger.

'You're surely not going to arrest me?' he said.

'You can't be that surprised,' Cassidy said, as Victor moved in to secure him.

Sykes shoved Victor aside to face up to Cassidy.

'You said you'd give me one chance, and I've taken it.'

'Except when you're around people die, and there comes a point when I have to ask how you've used that chance.'

Victor moved in again, and this time Sykes let him take his arms, but he dragged his heels as he was taken to the door.

'I helped you find Renard,' he shouted over his shoulder. 'I helped you explain what he was doing. I helped you explain the deaths in the jailhouse. What more could I do?'

'You could have stayed away from my town.'

Sykes treated Cassidy to one last glare and then Victor moved him out of the office, leaving Cassidy and Hearst alone.

'You promised me,' Hearst said, slapping Cassidy's shoulder, 'that you'd use the journey to work out what's the right thing to do, even if it's the wrong thing. I'm relieved you've done that.'

Cassidy frowned and looked through the barred window at the main drag. The two groups of aggrieved men had followed them here, but they were only talking amongst themselves.

'Actually, I decided to do the wrong thing, because that's the right thing to do.'

'Throwing Sykes in a cell isn't wrong.'

'Except it is. The more I learn, the more likely it looks that he didn't kill anyone.'

'We're in no position to judge what happened ten years ago, and what about the recent deaths?'

'They suggest that someone wants us to think Sykes killed them.' When Hearst looked sceptical, Cassidy lowered his voice. 'And I hate to say this, but the bank raid in Prudence wasn't all it seemed.'

Hearst sighed and tipped back his hat.

'Which makes me wonder why you've thrown him in a cell.'

'Because as I told Sykes, people die when he's around. Whether he's killing them or someone's making it look like he's killing them, it won't matter none to the victims.'

'I can see that.'

Cassidy beckoned Hearst to join him in looking out the window.

'Whether that's a good idea or not, I'm sure those men out there won't appreciate it.'

CHAPTER 12

'They're still watching the jailhouse,' Hearst said.

Cassidy raised his hat to consider Hearst, and then lowered it.

'Watching them won't change anything,' he said. He leaned back in his chair and placed his feet on the desk. 'So get some rest until the trouble starts up.'

The two lawmen had taken up residence in the jailhouse, presuming that the gathered gunmen would act before too long and the two jailers would struggle to repel them.

'When do you think that'll be?'

'I'd guess they'll come with the night.' Cassidy sighed. 'Which means I'll have to have a word with them before then.'

Cassidy still sat back in his chair enjoying a moment of peace before he clattered his feet down on the floor. He gestured at Hearst to stay put, and then headed to the door.

He stopped in the doorway and noted that both

groups had moved across the main drag. The larger group was loitering outside the Two Bit saloon while the other group was closer and standing beside the stable.

With the larger group forcing the customers to wend a path through them to reach the saloon and the small group merely leaning against the wall, Cassidy decided to speak to the larger group first. He moved past the men outside the stable and nodded to them, receiving blank stares from the four men in return.

Then he walked on to the saloon. As he approached, the men nudged each other and then swung round to face him.

Nine men were in this group and with the arrogance brought on by their superior numbers they considered him with smirks and murmured comments to each other. They formed into a line and that blocked the path of two men who were ahead of Cassidy, forcing them to walk past the saloon.

'You folks are causing a disturbance,' Cassidy said, gesturing at the departing men. 'Either enjoy the hospitality of the saloon or move on.'

'In that case I'll enjoy a drink in the saloon,' one man said after offering his name as Wilfred Dooley. 'Tell Sykes Caine to come and enjoy it with me.'

'I can't do that.' Cassidy walked up to Wilfred. 'Sykes is locked in the jailhouse.'

Wilfred raised an eyebrow in surprise. 'I thought he was your deputy.'

'He was, but I've arrested him.' Cassidy offered a smile. 'Since he returned to Monotony the bodies have been piling up again and that's too much of a coincidence for me.'

Wilfred looked at the others. They all returned surly glares and headshakes, so he stepped up closer to Cassidy.

'That's not good enough. Sykes got away with killing Peter Thornley ten years ago and now he'll answer for it.'

With one mystery resolved, Cassidy glanced over his shoulder. The other men, whom he presumed were friends of Gerald Norton, had moved on to loiter at the corner.

'As nobody has ever been charged for that crime, the case is still open and so if—'

'We're not interested in no excuses this time,' Wilfred muttered, shoving Cassidy's shoulder. 'Send Sykes out here and we'll take care of your case.'

'From what I've seen of Sykes, he'd take care of you. Now, move along or join him in jail.'

Wilfred snorted a laugh and looked at the nearest man to share his amusement. The moment that man laughed, he turned back, his fist rising to punch Cassidy's jaw, but Cassidy was aware of his likely response and he deflected the intended blow with a raised arm.

Then he grabbed Wilfred's wrist, turned him round and hurled him at the line of men. Wilfred barrelled into the nearest man, making them both fall over while the next two men stumbled. While he had the advantage, Cassidy backed away while waving a warning finger at the rest.

A click sounded to Cassidy's left and he turned to find the man at the end of the line had drawn his gun. With the gun already aimed at his chest, Cassidy faced him down, figuring he had no other option.

'I reckon,' the man said, 'you're the one who should move along.'

Wilfred got to his feet and drew his weapon, as did several other men, but he kept the gun aimed low. Then he blasted lead into the ground six inches from Cassidy's right boot.

Cassidy glanced down at the furrow in the ground and then back up at Wilfred.

'You have until sundown to leave town,' he said. 'I'll tell Sykes you were interested in his welfare.'

Then he turned on his heel, which made Wilfred hammer a second shot into the ground. This time Cassidy felt his heel kick. He paused before moving on.

'We end this, now,' Wilfred shouted after him.

Cassidy kept walking as Hearst emerged from the jailhouse. Cassidy nodded to him, indicating that he didn't want help.

He'd defined terms with these men and all he'd achieve by confronting them now was to provoke them into shooting him. As it was, when he reached the stable, a volley of lead tore out, the bullets ripping into the ground to either side of him.

This made the men whoop with delight and another volley tore out, this time splattering lead along the front of the stable. Cassidy speeded up before one of the gunmen holed him, either accidentally or not.

He moved towards the corner of the stable where the men who had been watching the altercation had now moved out of view. He wasn't sure if he should speak with the second group now, but that decision was taken out of his hands when the next blast sliced around his body and one bullet nicked his sleeve.

He swirled round to find the men were advancing on him with drawn guns ready to deliver on their ultimatum to end this stand-off now. Cassidy broke into a run and rounded the corner before the men could fire again, but then he skidded to a halt when he found the other group was facing him with guns drawn.

'You, too?' Cassidy said, noting that they hadn't aimed their guns at him.

'Those men might want to make Sykes pay for killing Peter Thornley,' one man said, 'but we'd like to thank him for killing Gerald Norton.'

Cassidy considered the men with surprise, but when they all nodded, he reckoned he'd take any help he could get. He smiled and turned back to the corner, and a moment later rapid footfalls sounded as the gunmen came closer.

Wilfred and another man came around the corner, their wide grins showing they expected to prevail with ease.

Their grins died when they found themselves facing five men with guns drawn. Wilfred dived for cover, but the other man raised his gun arm.

Before he could even aim at Cassidy, lead blasted into his chest from at least three men, making him stagger backwards for a pace before he toppled over. Any hope that this result would knock sense into the others fled when Wilfred shouted out an order for someone to head around the stable and come at them from the other side.

Cassidy ordered two men to head to the other corner to await the assault while he and the other two men stayed at the front corner. He listened for Wilfred shouting more instructions, but he heard nothing.

Then Hearst appeared at the corner of the jail-house. When he saw Cassidy, he shrugged.

Hearst would be able to see the front of the stable. So Cassidy looked around the corner to find Wilfred and the rest had gone.

He slapped the wall in irritation. The other two men didn't need any further telling and they moved off to the far corner to repel Wilfred.

Cassidy moved on to the stable door and glanced inside. He couldn't see anyone within, but Hearst was hurrying after him. He waited.

'Victor and Declan are confident they can keep

the gunmen out of the jailhouse,' Hearst said when he joined him.

'They'll have to get past us first,' Cassidy said, 'and we have help from an unexpected source.'

'I saw that, but the others all scooted around the stable.'

Cassidy nodded and they moved on to the corner. When the side of the stable proved to be clear, they hurried on.

The lawmen were a few paces from the back when gunfire erupted. Cassidy directed Hearst to move away from the corner to get a wider view on what was happening while he stopped at the corner.

He had just taken up his position when Hearst gestured and then hurried back, a volley of lead kicking at his heels speeding him on his way. Cassidy glanced around the corner with his gun held low to find that Wilfred was launching an assault at the other, but he'd left one man to deal with them.

The gunman turned his gun away from the fleeing Hearst to aim at Cassidy and Cassidy jerked back out of view. As a gunshot sprayed splinters inches from his face, cries of alarm sounded on the other side of the stable and Wilfred whooped in triumph. He was clearly getting the upper hand and that would give him a clear route to the jailhouse. With the need to act quickly, Cassidy gestured at Hearst to cover him and then broke into a run.

He came out into the open at speed while spraying

gunfire to his side. His sudden arrival surprised the gunman, who loosed off a wild shot, but by then Cassidy had got him in his sights.

While still running he hammered a shot into the gunman's shoulder that made him drop his gun and spin around. That moved him into Hearst's line of sight and the deputy dispatched him with a low shot to the stomach that dropped him.

Cassidy hunkered down and reloaded. Ahead, the gunfight was raging with Wilfred's men having taken refuge behind a cart they'd turned on its side while their opponents were pinned down in the open.

One of the gunmen glanced over his shoulder and when he saw one of their men lying face down in the dirt, he caught the attention of another man and both of them turned to Cassidy and Hearst. The others picked up on what had happened and they hurried around the side of the cart out of view while the other two blasted lead at the lawmen.

Cassidy aimed at the nearest man and they both got in a shot before Hearst caught the gunman in the leg, making him topple over to the side. The other man noted that he'd fallen and followed the others into cover beside the cart, but he managed only a single pace before both Hearst and Cassidy hammered a shot apiece into his side.

The man staggered, stumbled to the right, and then ploughed into the cart, which rocked as he slid down the wood to lie on his side. His death along with the lawmen's intervention gave their opponents heart.

Three men ran from the stable while firing on the run, keeping Wilfred's group down. Two men stopped to cover the third man, who moved on and then hunkered down to cover the other two.

With them acting in an organized manner Wilfred retaliated. He ran around the back of the cart aiming to gain an angle on them. He managed three paces before glancing over his shoulder, but nobody followed him. He slid to a halt and, while trapped out in the open, one of the men by the stable made him pay by slicing a shot into his left arm.

Wilfred went to one knee and then with grim determination he raised his gun to sight the shooter, but before he could fire, Cassidy shot at him. He'd taken careful aim and his only shot thundered into Wilfred's chest, making him twitch and then topple over to land face down in the dirt.

Cassidy waited until Hearst joined him and then they walked towards the cart. With Wilfred's men now trapped at the end of the cart and with the numbers being more even, Cassidy indicated to the men who had helped him to still their fire.

'Wilfred's bit the dirt,' he hollered, 'but you don't have to. Give up and you can have that meeting with Sykes, except it'll happen in the jailhouse.'

Hearst shot him an amused glance, clearly wondering if he was trying to goad them into fighting, or encouraging them to surrender. In truth he didn't mind which option they chose, but, as it turned out, one man hurled his gun over the cart and that encouraged the others to follow him.

In short order, the gunmen completed their surrender by coming out with their hands held high. Cassidy assessed the damage: three of Wilfred's men had been killed and one man had been wounded while one of the defenders had been killed, but when he'd escorted the surrendered men to the jailhouse, the defenders were in good spirits.

They offered to stay around town for a few days in case they were needed again. With the gunmen arrested and with no sign of further trouble erupting, Cassidy didn't think they would need to step in again, but he thanked them.

'Are we staying here?' Hearst asked, when Declan and Victor had dealt with the prisoners.

'We'll stay here until sundown,' Cassidy said. 'Then we'll return to the law office and resume normal duties.'

Hearst beamed at this and the lawmen settled down in the office to enjoy the rest of the afternoon. They were still feeling relaxed when Doc Taylor arrived.

Cassidy presumed he'd come to take care of the wounded prisoner and he called for Declan to deal with him, but Taylor shook his head.

'I'll see the prisoner later,' Taylor said. 'For now I have to spoil your good moods.'

121

Cassidy considered Taylor's sombre expression and winced.

'What's wrong?' he asked.

'I've just been shown another body. It's been lying behind the Shaw Hotel for a few hours, perhaps from before you got into that gunfight.' Taylor sighed. 'He's been killed in the same way as the others were.'

CHAPTER 13

'Anyone know who he is?' Cassidy asked when he and Hearst reached the back of the hotel.

Doc Taylor shook his head, but Hearst considered the man's face, and then nodded.

'I saw him with the gunslingers yesterday,' Hearst said, 'but he wasn't with them during the shootout today.'

'So he's similar to Gerald Norton.' Cassidy knelt down beside the body. 'And so is the nature of his dying.'

Bullet wounds marred the body's chest and furrows in the ground showed that he'd been dragged here after, presumably, being killed elsewhere. A scraped-out message was also on the ground, but Cassidy ignored it as he wondered what else he could learn from the scene.

'There's one thing that's different,' Hearst said with a gruff voice. 'This one can't be blamed on Sykes.'

Cassidy nodded. 'Finally proving that doesn't make this any easier, as people are still turning up dead.'

'If whoever did this was trying to frame Sykes, why kill when he's locked in the jailhouse?'

'Presumably because he didn't know that, which means he makes mistakes.' Cassidy threw open the body's jacket to consider the bullet holes.

'Although he didn't make any mistakes with his shooting.'

Cassidy nodded. 'This is impressive shooting. Could you shoot like that?'

'No. I could group bullets on a stationary target, but a person would drop after the first shot.' Hearst hunkered down beside Cassidy and pointed at each hole before nodding. 'Some or perhaps all of this must have been done after he'd been killed.'

'I agree, but why?'

Cassidy smiled, showing Hearst that he already had a theory. Hearst thought for a moment before replying.

'I guess because the killer wants us to know who killed them.'

Cassidy opened the body's shirt to display the wounds.

'Or maybe it's the opposite. The killer doesn't want us to know who killed them.'

Hearst frowned. 'I don't understand what you mean.'

'These wounds are distinctive, but maybe their

real purpose is to hide something. Did Volney's body have any distinctive marks on it?'

Hearst shrugged. 'He was different. For a start, he died in the jailhouse.'

'I know, but I'm starting to think both sets of deaths are linked.'

'In that case Volney had bruises on his chest.' Hearst raised an eyebrow as the idea took hold. 'Ossie had so many wounds it was hard to tell if any new ones were inflicted and Hamilton had just a head wound. Are you saying Webster had an accomplice outside the jail?'

'If I'm right, Webster was the accomplice, but either way, the men who died in jail couldn't have their wounds covered up, but these men could.'

Cassidy leaned closer and looked around the bullet wounds. With the blood and ragged holes he struggled to find anything conclusive, although between two of the holes he found a mark that looked like a burn.

He pointed it out to Hearst, who shrugged. Unable to learn anything more from the body, they moved on to the message. As before an extra word had been added.

'How like a god,' Hearst said, standing before the block of words. He sighed. 'It still don't make no sense, so sadly that probably means he plans to kill more people to complete it.'

'Unless we stop him first, which means I need to talk to someone who might know something about cryptic messages. While I find out what I can, head back to the jailhouse. Trouble is still likely to burst out there either from the inside or outside.'

'I don't know who could help you.' Hearst considered. 'Although this sounds like something Horace Franklyn would say.'

Cassidy nodded, but he said no more, not wanting to share his theory until he'd learnt everything he could. With that, they left Doc Taylor to deal with the body while they split up.

Cassidy headed out of town to Horace's house. In the early evening he'd expect Horace to be there, but he didn't answer his knock at the door.

As they hadn't spoken since he'd appointed Sykes as his deputy, Horace could be just ignoring him, so Cassidy opened the door. Standing in the corridor where last week he'd inadvertently burst in on Horace, he called out for him, but he heard nothing.

He figured he couldn't miss this opportunity to search his house and, making no attempt to be silent, so that if he was discovered he could claim he was looking for Horace, he moved from room to room. He wasn't sure what he hoped to find that would support his suspicion but when he reached the study and found a device that resembled the one he'd seen Horace use before, he examined it.

Unlike Horace's other device and the one in Prudence, it wasn't in a case. He didn't know how it worked, so it might have been his suspicious frame of mind, but it looked as if this one was more powerful.

It was larger with more cylinders, and other similar objects were around the room. He moved on to consider them and that drew his eye to a square shape etched into the floor. When he went to his knees to look closer, it turned out to be a trapdoor.

Being quiet now, he raised the door to find a cellar beneath with steps leading down, a chill emerging despite the warm early evening. He threw open the door fully to increase the available light, and he climbed down.

At the bottom the cellar had just enough height for him to stand upright. Standing in the rectangle of light from above he couldn't see the extent of the space, and the dank, putrid smell that seeped into his nostrils didn't encourage him to explore.

For long moments he didn't move and gradually he discerned that the cellar was larger than the study above. He edged forward, seeing two tables on which were laid out several more examples of Horace's device.

He stood between the tables and noted that on one table the devices had been dismantled and on the other they had been reassembled in a different configuration. He couldn't see the full extent of Horace's work, which would be intricate and required light, so he looked around for a lamp, and then he flinched.

A man was standing beyond the tables in the darkness.

Cassidy waited for him to make the first move, but when he didn't react, Cassidy's improving vision let him see the outlines of other men.

Now spooked, he turned around to find another man was behind him in the shadows. He, too, was standing still and this man was close enough for Cassidy to see that he'd never move again.

The man was long-dead, his clothes ragged and his form having become mummified. Rusted manacles secured the body to the wall and the man's jaw had dropped open perhaps from decay, although Cassidy couldn't help but think that the man had died screaming.

He examined the bodies on the other side of the table, and these were in the same state, manacled to the wall and mummified by time. He found ten men and he judged they had all been here for some time.

Decay ensured he couldn't recognize any of them. With the fading light reducing his chances of learning anything more here, he turned to the trapdoor to find that another man he'd not noticed before was beside the steps.

Numbed by what he'd discovered he shuffled closer and even when this man moved, he was slow to react. Then a metal bar came slicing through the air towards his head and he jerked away, but not before it caught him a glancing blow to the forehead.

He dropped to the floor, his vision swimming. Through pained eyes he caught glimpses of Horace looming over him, and in his disorientated state the mummified bodies appeared to surround him and help Horace secure him.

Then darkness stole over him.

A timeless period later a slap to the cheek dragged him back to consciousness. He was now sitting up and Horace was standing over him.

Cassidy struggled to focus as Horace moved something closer to his head. Then he turned away.

Cassidy shook himself, trying to regain full awareness, but he was tied up and couldn't move. As Horace climbed the steps out of the cellar, Cassidy's blurred vision still let him see the bodies that surrounded him, their silent and unseeing vigil letting him know that this was how it had ended for them, too.

Then Horace reached the study and slammed the trapdoor back into place. Darkness descended.

When Renard Icke woke up with a start, Victor was standing over him. Before Renard could become fully awake, Victor had dragged him off his cot, turned him around, and slammed him into the bars.

With his face mashed up against cold metal, Renard noted with a rueful grunt that this was how he'd secured Webster, but that had gone badly. Since then, his failure had depressed him and he'd fallen asleep and failed again.

Sykes Caine was in the adjoining cell. He'd told him that Webster had been arrested, but Webster had an accomplice and presumably that man was Victor. Then Renard heard scuffling in the next cell and he changed that assumption to the other jailer, Declan, also being involved.

They must have gone into their cells in a co-ordinated move, but Sykes had been more alert than Renard was and was fighting back. He didn't appear to have any more success as a grunt of pain sounded and the scuffling sounds stopped.

Declan marched Sykes out of the cell while holding him securely from behind. He brought Sykes into Renard's cell and stood him up against the bars beside Renard.

The two prisoners glanced at each other. With Sykes looking bemused, Renard shot him an apologetic look before he put his thoughts to how he could use this unexpected second chance. He relaxed, ensuring that when the jailers did their worst he'd be ready to retaliate, but neither man tried anything.

Confirmation of what they were waiting for came when footfalls sounded down the corridor, the paces slow and echoing. Like before, when the man turned the corner he tapped the bars, maintaining a steady pace until he came into view.

Renard had seen this man before when he'd been searching for Laidley, and Sykes confirmed his identity with a muttered comment.

'Horace Franklyn,' he said, 'what do you want with us?'

Horace held a case in one hand and a wooden handle with a metal tip in the other. He ignored Sykes as he tapped the bars, ensuring he touched every third bar until he entered the cell.

Then he moved behind Renard and a thud and a click sounded as he placed the case on the floor and opened it. Rustling and creaks sounded, but Renard couldn't work out what he was doing.

Horace must have given a silent order as Declan drew Sykes away from the bars. Sykes struggled, but Declan had a firm grip so Renard reckoned this was his best opportunity to act.

He tensed, preparing to try to free himself, but Victor was prepared for this eventuality and he grabbed the back of his head and jerked it forward. Renard's forehead thudded into a cell bar, the sound reverberating in his head and making him lose his balance.

The next he knew, Victor was bundling him back to his cot and he was too weak and disorientated to fight back. Ropes were wrapped around his wrists and ankles without him being able to even slow down the process.

When he shook off his numbness, he was tied to the cot and Horace was standing over him.

' "Look here upon this picture",' Horace said, ' "and on this, the counterfeit presentment of two brothers." '

131

'What does that mean?' Renard murmured grog-gily.

Horace turned away, leaving Victor standing guard over him.

'I reckon he means that you're next,' Victor said.

Renard looked past Horace to find that Sykes had been secured on the other cot in the same manner as he was, although his shirt had been ripped open to bare his chest. On the floor beside Sykes was Horace's case.

Metal cylinders were inside, the like of which Renard had never seen before, and Horace had connected the handle to them.

' "All that live must die",' Horace said, holding up the handle.

'So it was you ten years ago,' Sykes said, 'and that's all you were trying to say.'

'That's all anyone needs to say. We all live and we all die. So nothing matters.'

'I'd sooner work to make life better for the living than kill other people.'

'Reacting to what other people do isn't a noble ambition. I'm trying to make life better for the living by changing man's very soul.'

Horace pressed the end of the handle to Sykes's chest, making him buck and squirm. Horace waited until he stopped moving and then moved the handle to a lower position on his chest.

Again he pressed it down and again Sykes bucked, but he didn't make a sound even though

Renard heard a buzzing noise and he smelt burning. It took four more touches before Sykes cried out.

'How can this torture change a man's soul?' Sykes muttered.

Horace withdrew a sheet of paper from his case and made a note.

' "When the blood burns, how prodigal the soul".' Horace shrugged. 'I may fail again to uncover the secrets of a man's nature, but now that I have this device I'll work on this scientifically until I find out how I can gentle a man.'

'How many have died for this *scientific* work?'

'Not enough yet, I fear, and what you've endured so far was the lowest level.' Horace reached down and moved something in the case. 'This will be the middle setting.'

Horace stood up and regarded Sykes as he planned where to place the handle next.

'You've lied and cheated to cover up what you've been doing,' Sykes said. 'But why frame me to take the blame?'

' "This brave o'erhanging firmament," ' Horace said, ignoring him, ' "this majestical roof, fretted with golden fire. Why, it appears no other thing to me than a foul and pestilent congregation of vapours." '

'What in tarnation are you talking about?' Sykes shouted.

' "What a piece of work is man. How noble in

133

reason, how infinite in faculty. In form and moving how express and admirable. In action how like an angel." ' Horace leaned over Sykes and placed the handle above his heart. ' "In apprehension how like a god!" '

Then he pressed the handle down on Sykes's chest.

CHAPTER 14

Cassidy strained against the bonds that secured him, but he could move only a few inches. In the darkness he couldn't work out how he'd been tied up, but he knew he was sitting on a chair with his hands behind his back and with a gag over his mouth.

His last sight before Horace had closed the trap-door was of the tables on either side of him and that gave him hope. The devices Horace had been constructing had metal objects and if he could bring one to hand, he might find a sharp edge he could use.

He started his attempt to free himself by rocking the chair from side to side, hoping to walk it closer to a table. His first attempt failed to move the chair and he succeeded only in wriggling, which after his blow to the head made him feel light-headed.

He waited until the discomfort passed and tried again. This time he raised a chair leg for a moment before it thudded back down, but having now worked out how he should distribute his weight, he rocked to the right.

Something cold brushed against his cheek, making his teeth rattle and pain shoot down his neck. If he'd not been gagged, he'd have shouted out.

He sat still and it took him several moments to identify the odd feeling as being the same as the shock that he'd experienced when he'd touched the metal end of a handle in Horace's device. Clearly Horace had placed one of those handles beside his face in case he should try to escape.

Accordingly, he rocked the chair to the left and this time he moved only a fraction before his jaw touched another handle. He grunted in pain and jerked his head away, only for the back of his head to hit a third device.

He tensed to avoid moving and he smelt a whiff of burning that he presumed was his hair. He figured Horace had probably left another handle in front of his head, but in the darkness he couldn't be sure.

He steeled himself to confirm this, but he couldn't move as he sat paralyzed by fear of what might be close to him in the darkness. That thought made him recall what he'd already seen in the cellar.

Unless he escaped he'd join the other bodies down here permanently, so he shuffled forward. Sure enough, something pressed against his forehead.

A jolt of pain sliced through his head, the metal end so close he saw a spark. He jerked backwards, knocking him into the handle behind him.

The second jolt made him lose control of his body and he twitched and squirmed in the chair as if the handles were still touching him. When the twitching stopped, he continued to flinch for several minutes.

Curiously, despite the discomfort, the troubling experience heartened him. Other than the momentary pain and the shock of the unexpected, he didn't reckon he'd suffered any permanent damage.

He resolved to resume his attempt to move the chair and ignore the devices that were around him. He kept his head as still as possible while rocking the chair and he managed three movements to the right before he touched a handle.

Although he'd tensed in anticipation, he still flinched so strongly his head jerked away, making his jaw crash into the handle to his left. With the shock numbing his muscles, he was unable to control his movements and he stayed pressed up against the metal end sending repeated jolts through his jaw and neck.

Then something gave way and the handle fell away from him. The next he knew he was falling over.

Clattering sounded as he hit the floor on his side. The contraptions fell on top of him and he lay twitching, lost in a dark hell.

Every time he moved away from one jolt, he pressed against another handle, making him flinch again and touch another one. He fought for control and by degrees he stopped himself moving.

He lay, breathing shallowly, trying to work out whether he'd improved his situation. By flexing his legs and arms, he discovered that the handles, along with wires and several other objects, were lying across his body. As getting access to Horace's devices was what he'd wanted to achieve, he felt heartened enough to risk moving further. To his delight this didn't result in any more shocks and, even better, his squirming must have loosened his bonds as he could move his limbs with greater freedom.

He felt around with his hands and although he couldn't touch anything, one of the handles pressed against the crook of his elbow. He didn't receive a shock, so the wooden length must be touching him. It was lying between his arms and the chair, having slipped down when he fell.

He drew his arms towards his body and that pressed the handle against the back of the chair, producing a promising creaking sound. He exerted more pressure, generating another creak.

The motion made another metal end touch his chest. He flinched away, but he couldn't get away from it and the metal continued to jolt him. He tensed, getting another jolt, and then a loud creak sounded followed by a snapping sound.

He slumped forward and his forehead pressed up against a table leg. He felt sure that the additional movement was a good thing, but the repeated shocks had numbed his body.

Only when a clattering sounded and a handle fell against his leg did he move again. When he found he could move more than before, he kicked out, sending pieces of broken chair and rope flying. Then he fought his way to his feet, thankfully without getting any more shocks, and stood free. He caught his breath and moved forward tentatively.

Debris cluttered around his feet and he kicked it away until he nudged into a table. He stopped and focused on the faint rectangle of light in the ceiling that marked the trapdoor.

He walked around the table keeping one hand on the wood and by the time he approached the door, he was walking with ease as his muscles relaxed. He stumbled once when he reached the steps, but then, eager to escape, he scrambled up the steps and put a hand to the door.

The trapdoor hadn't been secured so he pushed it open, letting more light filter down. He emerged from the cellar and then came to a sudden halt.

A man was standing in a shaft of moonlight shining down through the study window. The man's face was in shadow, but he could see enough of his body to see the gun he'd aimed at him.

'Reach,' the man said.

Cassidy started to raise his hands, but he stopped when he recognized the voice. He laughed, accepting the shocks must have muddled his senses for him not to have recognized Tormond.

'It's me, Cassidy,' he said.

Tormond moved forward so that the moonlight revealed his face and when Cassidy moved into the light he looked at him with surprise.

'What are you doing here?' he asked, holstering his gun.

'I could ask you the same.'

Tormond frowned. 'I'd guess you had the same thought as I'd had, that the cryptic message beside the last body is something Horace might have said.'

'I did, and there's more. I reckon he shot holes in the recent bodies to cover up the damage his contraption made.'

'I can't see his device doing any good, but I can't see it causing no harm either.'

'The one everyone's seen wouldn't, but he's built bigger devices.' Cassidy rubbed his jaw and hands ruefully. 'I can believe that repeatedly using them on somebody would kill them.'

Tormond sighed. 'I've known Horace for years. I'll find it harder to accept he's guilty than to accept Sykes is innocent.'

'In that case, look in the cellar.' Cassidy gulped. 'You were a lawman longer than I've been, and you've seen some terrible sights, but this one takes

140

some stomaching.'

Tormond busied himself with finding an oil lamp and lighting it. Then, with a stern expression on his face, he headed down into the cellar.

While he was gone, Cassidy sat down and rubbed his arms and legs, confirming that he'd escaped from his ordeal unscathed aside from the occasional twitch. Tormond took his time and when he emerged he joined Cassidy in sitting.

'I reckon he tortured the older bodies,' he said. 'Then he covered up their injuries with gunshots, but those who were too badly marked he kept down there.'

'Then recently he acquired his present device,' Cassidy said, 'and that let him continue his work while causing less damage.'

Tormond nodded. 'I recognized only one of them. I can't remember his name, but he had an ugly scar where someone had shot away part of his chin. There's enough of him left to see that. He looks like he's been there the longest.'

'Who was he?'

'He rode into town and raised hell about twelve years ago.' Tormond considered Cassidy. 'He picked a fight with several people, including Horace.'

'And Horace retaliated and he ended up down there.' Cassidy felt the back of his hand, fingering the healed burn as well as checking he was no longer twitching. 'It's possible the rest were no-good types

141

who were passing through.'

Tormond nodded. 'Men who weren't here long enough for anyone to miss them.'

'Except for the ones who ended up in jail.' Cassidy looked aloft as he pieced together the situation. 'Horace is wealthy, so when he visited Prudence he bribed Webster to give him access to men he viewed as worthless. Then Webster came here and they carried on the arrangement.'

'It fits together, except for his daughter Availia. She wasn't like the others.'

'Whatever the answer about her, we have to find Horace.'

Tormond grunted that he agreed and they wasted no time before hurrying out of the house. Once they were outside, Cassidy stopped. Tormond walked on for a few paces and then beckoned him on.

'We have to hurry,' Tormond said.

Cassidy set his hands on his hips. 'We do, but answer me one thing first: did Sykes rob Prudence's bank?'

Tormond stopped and looked skyward for a moment.

'We haven't got the time to talk about that.'

'We have, because I just need a simple yes or no.'

'The answer isn't as simple as that, and you know my record as a lawman. I always found the guilty and now I intend to help you finally conclude my one unsolved case.'

Tormond met Cassidy's eye and urged him to join him, but Cassidy shook his head.

'Answer the question.'

Tormond spread his hands and sighed.

'The teller, Luke Edwards, suspected another corrupt teller was stealing from the bank, so he set a trap. As the operation had to be carried out in secret and I was an old and trusted friend, I helped him.'

'Sykes was the only one arrested.'

'That's because the other teller was Yancy Dix, the first body to turn up.' Tormond's shoulders slumped. 'Peter Thornley was a bank raider who tried to raid the bank. Even Availia Franklyn had taught at a school in Prudence. Everything suggested a wider conspiracy and afterwards it looked as if Sykes had been at the heart of it.'

'For the last time, answer the question.'

Tormond moved back to join Cassidy and he looked him in the eye.

'I didn't frame Sykes, but Luke did. With Peter and Yancy dead, he thought Sykes was involved. I only found out what he'd done after Sykes had been found guilty. My crime was not to do anything about it.'

'That's no justification.'

'The bodies had stopped turning up, so I found that I could live with it.'

'And now?'

'And now I'll help you to find Horace. Then I'll

tell the truth, no matter what it does to my reputation.'

Cassidy nodded and then moved on past
Tormond, who dallied for a moment before joining
him. On the way back to town they didn't discuss
the situation again.

Cassidy tried to put his disappointment at
Tormond's actions aside and thought back through
everything he knew about Horace, hoping he would
recall something that would let him find him before
he could kill again.

Tormond's face was thunderous, appearing lost
in his own private torment.

When they stopped outside the law office,
Tormond headed to the Two Bit saloon while
Cassidy moved on to the jailhouse to collect Hearst.
He resolved to decide whether or not he would seek
Sykes's help when he met him.

These concerns fled from his thoughts when he
entered the office and found Hearst slumped over
his desk. He hurried to his side and found a dark
bruise on the side of his head, but he was breathing
shallowly. Cassidy ran back to the door.

Tormond was emerging from the saloon with his
posture hunched, but when he saw Cassidy gesture
to him, he broke into a run. By the time he arrived,
Cassidy had cautiously opened the door to the cells.

He could hear nothing beyond, which was odd as
Victor and Declan should be on duty, and they
ought to have reacted to the door opening. He

waited for Tormond to join him and they moved on down a short corridor. When they reached the end where it branched into two, they stopped. The jail-house was laid out with cells facing the branching corridors. The prisoners from the aborted assault were in the cells to the right, while Sykes and Renard had been placed to the left. Cassidy could see down both corridors. Victor and Declan weren't visible.

He moved to the right until he could see into the first cell. The prisoners were either lying on their cots or pacing, and there was no suggestion they had been disturbed.

Tormond ventured down the other corridor, but he stopped after a few paces and signalled for Cassidy's attention. When Cassidy joined him, he saw that the two cell doors at the end of the corridor were open.

Cassidy moved into the lead and walked on cautiously until he could see into the first cell, which was empty. A wall separated the cell from the last one and even before Cassidy could see into it he noted changes in the light level that showed people were moving around inside.

He drew his gun and at his shoulder Tormond matched his action. Then, with a firm stride and while not attempting to move quietly, he stepped forward to face the cell.

It took him a moment to work out what was happening inside as Victor and Declan had their backs to him and they were blocking most of his view. His footfalls made them turn, revealing that Renard and Sykes had been tied to their cots with gags over their mouths, while Horace stood over Sykes with two handles from his device held over Sykes's chest.

Horace looked over his shoulder and then, with a lunge, he pressed the handles down on Sykes's skin, making him buck. The device was larger than the ones in the cellar and Cassidy flinched in sympathy for Sykes's plight before he rushed forward.

His momentary shock let Tormond react first and he reached the doorway before him. Declan moved to confront him, but Tormond brushed past him and paced up to Horace.

As Cassidy followed him into the cell and knocked Victor aside, Tormond grabbed Horace's shoulder and hurled him across the cell where he slammed into the wall.

While Sykes continued to twitch on his cot, Horace turned round. He had kept hold of one of the handles and he brandished it as a weapon, but Tormond ignored him as he held Sykes down.

When he failed to stop Sykes from twitching, he tore the ropes from his wrists. Cassidy turned his gun on Horace, making Horace lower the handle and then toss it to the floor, his disgusted expression acknowledging it was of no use when confronting a man with a gun.

With Cassidy's attention not on them, Declan and Victor took the opportunity to scramble away.

Within moments they had scurried outside and then down the corridor, but Cassidy was watching Horace and he let them go.

Only when Tormond tore the gag from Sykes's mouth did Sykes stop squirming and, while taking deep breaths, he looked up at Tormond.

'I don't know what I can say,' Tormond said, his voice gruff.

'You've done enough already,' Sykes said between gasps.

Sykes glanced at Horace and then with quick movements he freed himself from the last of the rope and tried to get up. He failed to get off the cot so Tormond helped him stand.

'It probably won't help you none to hear this,' Cassidy said, 'but I threw you in a cell because I thought that would uncover the truth. It seems it did.'

'You're right,' Sykes murmured. 'It doesn't help.'

Sykes indicated to Tormond that he could stand unaided. Then he shuffled across the cell to Renard's side and started work on his bonds.

'I've been to Prudence and heard some of your story, Renard,' Cassidy said, when Sykes had removed Renard's gag. 'I accept more is going on here than I first thought, so I'm prepared to hear your side of the story.'

Renard acknowledged Cassidy and then nodded at the ropes around his wrists. His easy movement suggested that Horace had yet to torture him.

147

Cassidy gestured to Horace for him to leave the cell while backing into the doorway. The moment he stepped into the corridor a gunshot blasted, rattling into the bars and making Cassidy jerk back.

He looked around, confirming that nobody inside had fired, and then glanced through the doorway. This time he didn't invite a gunshot, but in his brief look he saw that Victor had hunkered down at the end of the corridor and he'd fired at him.

Worse, Declan was moving down the other corridor and he was opening the cells.

CHAPTER 15

'The men you arrested today are in those cells,' Tormond said, when Cassidy reported what was happening outside.

'And they were hell-bent on shooting up Sykes,' Cassidy said.

'Let them have Horace,' Sykes said. 'That might placate them.'

'Enough people have suffered because of his actions. His only function now is to provide answers.'

Cassidy beckoned Tormond to watch over Horace while he took up a position in the doorway, but Tormond shook his head.

'Sykes can take care of Horace,' he said. 'You need another gun.'

Sykes directed an appreciative glance at Tormond. Then, while Tormond joined Cassidy in the doorway, he abandoned trying to work out how Renard's bonds had been tied and moved over to control Horace.

'We need to seize control of this situation before Declan frees all the prisoners,' Cassidy said. 'You take this side of the corridor. I'll take the other.'

He waited until Tormond nodded and then hurried out of the cell. He pressed himself to the wall while peering down the corridor to find that Victor was following him with his gun.

Behind Victor, Declan was working his way down the cells and several men had spilled out into the corridor. These men dived for cover when they saw Cassidy raise his gun.

Victor loosed off a shot that clattered into the wall four feet ahead of Cassidy. Before he could fire again, Tormond emerged from the cell and that spooked him into scurrying for cover.

Cassidy hurried him on his way with a gunshot that kicked at his heels. When Victor disappeared around the corner, Cassidy had an uninterrupted view of the other corridor.

Declan wasn't visible and so he started walking. Tormond matched his pace although he moved closer to the wall as they passed each cell to give him some cover.

Beyond the corner, the prisoners edged out into the corridor. Cassidy gestured at them to get back in the cells, but the first ones had come out to appraise the scene and they beckoned to the other prisoners.

A moment later Webster Todd led a block of prisoners into the corridor. They had no weapons but several men had removed their boots and were waving them above their heads while the next wave had tin plates which they rattled against the wall.

There were at least a dozen men, but even with Webster urging them on, only a few were the gunmen who had wanted to shoot up Sykes, and Cassidy didn't want to be forced into mowing them down. So he fired into the ceiling as a warning, but that didn't slow them down.

Instead, the leading men hurled their boots and plates at them, forcing Tormond and Cassidy to flinch away. When Cassidy turned back, he found that the missiles had been only a distraction. Using a surprisingly organized move, the leading men dropped to their knees to reveal Declan with his gun brandished.

Victor chose that moment to slip around the corner and he picked out Tormond while Declan aimed at Cassidy. Tormond reacted with efficient speed and he slammed a high shot into Victor's chest that toppled him over backwards into the prisoners behind him.

Cassidy matched his speed and sliced a low shot into Declan's stomach that made him stumble into the corner. Declan wasted a shot into the wall before he fell over on to his side.

Before Cassidy and Tormond could congratulate themselves the prisoners swarmed over the fallen men, and on the run Webster gathered up Declan's dropped gun.

Clearly Webster hoped the prisoners could over-come their adversaries by weight of numbers. Cassidy and Tormond aimed at the front line, but they didn't fire in the hope that they'd relent.

The men kept moving and when they'd halved the distance to them, Cassidy fired at the man who had picked up Victor's gun. He hit him in the chest and he tumbled over.

A moment later Tormond dispatched a man running along his side of the corridor near to Webster, although Cassidy presumed he'd been aiming at Webster. This still didn't slow the rest and they came pounding on, forcing them to continue firing.

Cassidy dispatched another man with a low shot to the stomach, but the man kept running on for several paces before he fell over. Then he keeled into Cassidy and they both went down.

Cassidy floundered beneath the man's dead weight and by the time he'd thrown him aside and stood up, he was surrounded. A prisoner punched him in the stomach while another delivered a flail-ing blow to his cheek that sent him spinning into the wall.

One man pinned him to the wall while the other man tried to wrest the gun from his hand, but Cassidy kept a tight grip of the weapon. When the man raised Cassidy's arm, Cassidy sliced a deadly shot into the man's chest, making him fold over and drop to the floor.

The second man released his hold to flinch away from the gun, but he wasn't fast enough to avoid Cassidy turning his gun arm to the side. He dispatched him with a low shot and then looked beyond the man's falling form to see how Tormond was faring.

The former lawman had killed another prisoner. Cassidy noted he was the man who had been shot in the leg earlier and was the last of the men who had arrived in town with Wilfred.

The other prisoners had no motive other than a desire to use the situation to escape. So, after joining in the charge, the fight went out of them and they edged away.

'Go back to your cells,' Tormond said. 'You've had your fun.'

The prisoners rocked back and forth, clearly torn between self-preservation and the hope of escape. When Cassidy turned his gun on them, their shoulders slumped.

'Deal with them,' Cassidy said. 'I'll get Horace.'

Tormond gestured and the prisoners moved off in a subdued manner, letting Cassidy consider the fallen. He counted the men he'd taken prisoner earlier and these men were now dead, but then with a thudding heart he realized he hadn't accounted for one of their opponents.

Webster wasn't amongst the fallen.

He gestured at the prisoners, urging them to hurry to give the impression he wasn't concerned.

Then he pivoted on his right leg and swirled around while moving to the side.

As he'd feared, Webster had slipped into one of the cells and he had a gun aimed at him. Cassidy's sudden movement took him by surprise and when he fired, his gunshot flew a few inches wide of Cassidy's chest, while Cassidy hammered a shot that took a deflection off a bar before slamming into Webster's right hip.

Webster stumbled into the corridor only for Tormond to turn and tear a gunshot into his chest that made him topple over sideways.

'Always keep count,' Tormond said with a wink, before he moved on after the prisoners.

Cassidy smiled and walked back to the end cell, but when it came into view, he saw that Sykes was now holding a gun on Horace.

'Where did you get that?' he called out.

Sykes glanced at him through the bars.

'I took it off Horace, and I'm about to let him have it back.'

When Cassidy could see into the corner of the cell, Renard was still secured to his cot while Horace had taken advantage of the chaos to stand beside him. He now held a handle above his temple.

'If you tighten that trigger finger,' Horace said, 'I'll press the handle against Renard's head. Death will be instantaneous.'

Cassidy joined Sykes in the cell, making Horace swing round to flash a warning glare at him.

'What do you want?' Cassidy said, stopping in the corridor.

'To leave this place,' Horace said.

'I've been in your cellar. You know I can't let you do that.'

'You do remember all the circumstances? You should be grateful for what I've done. Think of the trouble those men could have caused you if I hadn't got to them before they could do their worst.'

Cassidy shook his head while edging forward so that he could get a clear shot at Horace through the bars.

'You were the one causing the most trouble in Monotony.'

Horace waved the handle at Cassidy before moving it back to Renard.

'I only took the worst of the worst.'

'Yet you're threatening Renard. From what I've learned about him, he was only looking for revenge as he tried to work out who killed his brother, which was you.'

Renard provided a brief nod, but Horace dismissed the matter with a wave of his free hand.

'I tried to cure his brother, like the others. Being evil is a sickness of the soul and it can be cured like any sickness of the body. I've worked hard and now that I have this device I'm getting close to uncovering the secret that'll improve all our futures.'

'All I saw was a lot of dead men who died in agony.'

155

'I regretted the pain I had to cause, but it was a price I was prepared to pay.'

'Was Barney Rose prepared to pay that price?'

'He was in a bad way when I found him.'

'Then what about your daughter Availia?' Cassidy asked, assuming hers was one death Horace couldn't dismiss.

Darkness clouded Horace's features.

'She didn't deserve that, but I hardened my heart. She'd ignored my instructions and gone down into the cellar. She saw what was down there. I couldn't risk my secret getting out.'

This revelation made Cassidy glare at Horace in amazement, as did Sykes. Even Renard ignored his predicament to look at him with horror.

Horace considered Renard and it might have been Renard's expression, but Horace relaxed his hand, letting the handle slip away from him.

Sykes noticed his apparent change of heart and he moved forward to grab him, but that ended Horace's brief reflective moment and with a cry of defiance he plunged the handle down at Renard's head.

Cassidy fired at Horace's chest a second before the metal end touched Renard's skin, veering Horace's aim so that he caught Renard only a glancing blow before he fell.

Sykes swept the handle away from Renard, who lay rigidly so presumably the metal part hadn't touched him. Cassidy hurried into the cell while keeping his gun on Horace, but Horace lay on his chest.

Cassidy knelt beside him and turned him over on to his back to find his eyes were already unfocused.

' "Give me your pardon, sir," ' Horace murmured, a weak hand rising to him. ' "I've done you wrong." '

'Sure can't do that,' Cassidy said.

Horace exhaled his breath with a long sigh and the hand flopped down to the floor.

' "Oh, I die", Cassidy.'

Horace's head rocked to the side and when he didn't move again, Cassidy stood up.

'Good riddance, you evil varmint,' he said.

'And may flights of devils welcome thee to your rest,' Sykes said.

CHAPTER 16

'Horace kept records,' Hearst said, when he and Sykes emerged from the cellar. 'So we should be able to work out who all the dead men were.'

Both men's faces were ashen, and Cassidy directed them to head outside and get some fresh air.

While Cassidy had worked out the extent of Horace's activities, he had kept information on what was in the house private with only the lawmen along with Tormond and Doc Taylor knowing the details.

Later he planned to return to Prudence to gather the rest of the details of Horace's actions there, as well as questioning Luke Edwards about the conspiracy over the fictitious bank raid ten years ago.

He would also have to work out if Renard had gone too far in his quest for revenge, and if Tormond's actions had been justified. He was pleased that he would only have to collect the evidence while a judge would have to decide on their guilt.

Whatever the answer to all these questions, he feared that Horace's activities weren't just confined to these towns. He had been well travelled and he'd never heard a bad word spoken against a man who had probably killed more men than any outlaw Cassidy had ever faced.

He figured that once the news got out, the reaction to the man whom everyone had thought was Sykes would be replicated and an angry mob would descend on the house. If they tried to burn it down, Cassidy reckoned he'd let them. If nothing else, directing their ire at Horace might help to convince everyone that they'd wronged Sykes.

'Horace kept meticulous notes of what he did with his victims,' Sykes said, when they were standing outside. 'He had no success with his plan to change a man's soul, but should Doc Taylor read them?'

'Taylor is a real doctor,' Cassidy said. 'He'd have no use for Horace's ravings.'

Sykes nodded and the three men stood in silence.

'I was wrong about you, Sykes,' Hearst said after a while. 'Even if you can't accept my apology, at least I learnt that I ought to judge a man by his actions and not by his reputation.'

Sykes sighed. 'I waited ten years for someone to

say that. Perhaps when I've heard it a few more times, I might work out what I should say in return.'

'Don't say anything,' Hearst said. 'I did wrong, not you.'

When Sykes nodded, Cassidy slapped Hearst on the back and then stood before Sykes. He had already apologized to him and so he concentrated on the other important matter.

'Does that mean you're staying around to hear those apologies?'

Sykes nodded. 'Even if you never knew it, Horace was reducing the trouble you faced, so I reckon you'll need my help in the future.'

'I reckon I will,' Cassidy said with a smile.

Then the three men turned to face west and the setting sun. The sky was a deep red almost to the zenith.

'Horace was wrong,' Sykes said. 'An evening like this makes you feel good to be alive, even if we all must die one day.'

Cassidy shrugged. 'Speak for yourself. I intend to live for ever.'

The two deputies laughed and with that, they headed back to town.